THE **SYDING**

ADVENTURES

PIRATES

AND

PRISONERS

WRITTEN BY — 2 — MARY WEEKS MILLARD

DayOne

© Day One Publications 2013

First printed 2013

ISBN 978-1-84625-365-2

All Scripture quotations are from the **New International Version** 1984
Copyright © 1973, 1978, 1984

Published by Day One Publications
Ryelands Road, Leominster, HR6 8NZ

TEL 01568 613 740 FAX 01568 611 473

email—sales@dayone.co.uk

UK web site—www.dayone.co.uk

USA web site—www.dayonebookstore.com

This book is entirely a work of fiction. Some actual place names have been used, but the names of all people and the villages where they live are entirely fictitious.

Printed by TJ International Ltd

Dedication

To Joe, my wonderful helper in fundraising for the children of Rwanda. Continue to love and serve the Lord.

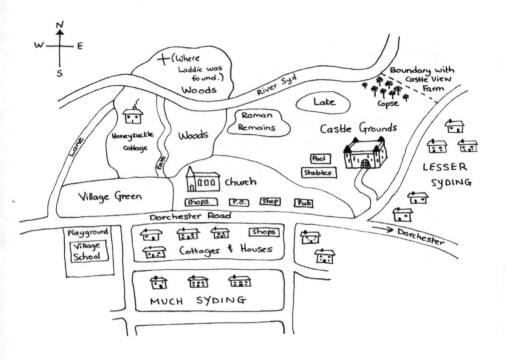

N
W — E
S

+ (Where Laddie was found.)

Woods

River Syd

Boundary with Castle View Farm

Lake

Copse

Honeysuckle Cottage

Woods

Roman Remains

Castle Grounds

Lane

Farm

Pool

Stables

LESSER SYDING

Village Green

Church

Shops   P.O.   Shop   Pub

Dorchester Road

→ Dorchester

Playground

Village School

Shops

Cottages & Houses

MUCH SYDING

Map of Much Syding

Acknowledgements and thanks

I wish to express my grateful thanks to Tirzah Jones, Director of Youth Ministries of DayOne, Chris Jones and all the editorial staff for their help with this manuscript.

To Malcolm, my ever patient and encouraging husband and to my kind friends who have taken the time to read and comment on this book.

Chapter One

It was the end of the summer holidays. Theo and his great friend Tyler were looking forward to spending the last day together before the new term began. They had mixed feelings about going to the comprehensive school in the nearby town of Dorchester. It would be such a big change after attending Much Syding village school. Both boys had started there just a year ago and had found the first months very difficult, but in the end they had loved it. Now it was all change yet again.

Theo lived at Syding Castle, which his mother ran as a bed and breakfast business. They had been very busy through the summer, and Theo, along with his brother and sisters (Penny who was sixteen, the twins Sebastian and Felicity who were thirteen), had needed to help their mum. However, she had promised Theo that this last day was to be a day off so that he could go to the beach with Tyler. Tyler's father had promised to take them to a quiet, rocky beach called Osmington so that they could explore using Theo's metal detector.

Theo called out goodbye to his mum, then got on his bike and rode from his home in Lesser Syding over to the cottage in the woods where Tyler lived. He always loved going there. Tyler lived with his parents and baby sister and his

gran next door in her Romany caravan or 'vardo' as it was
called. Although they were Romany gypsies, they no longer
travelled from place to place but had settled in Honeysuckle
Cottage at the edge of Much Syding woods. Tyler's dad
worked for the forestry commission and looked after the
woods. He knew so much about flora and fauna and had
taught Tyler to love the natural world. Tyler already knew he
wanted to be a conservationist when he grew up!

"Hi, Theo," called his friend as he arrived at the cottage;
"Leave your bike in the shed; Dad is almost ready, and Mum
has made us a mountain of sandwiches. She always says
the sea air gives me an appetite! I hope you remembered to
bring your detector."

"Of course I did!" answered Theo. "Let's hope we find
something more than bottle tops today."

Soon the boys were in the car and speeding on their way
to Osmington. They drove through the old village with
its quaint thatched cottages and down a narrow lane to a
hamlet called Osmington Mills. The hamlet ended abruptly
with an old smugglers' inn and then a steep path down to
the beach. They parked the car and scrambled down the
path. Not many people were around, even though it was
a warm day. The tide was a long way out, so there were
numerous rock pools to investigate. Tyler's dad, Bill, was in
his element splashing around the pools looking for wildlife.
It was amazing how many species lived in the shallow water.

In no time at all it was lunchtime, and they sat on a large rock in the sunshine and ate their sandwiches. Everyone was hungry! Afterwards Bill told the boys they could go off with the metal detector while he had a snooze in the sun but warned them to be careful of slipping on the wet rocks and also to watch the tide as it was on the turn.

"Ok, Dad," shouted Tyler as he and Theo headed off to explore the beach, hoping they would reach the next cove of Ringstead by climbing over the rocks and then walking back over the headland.

They had been clambering for a while when they saw pieces of wood, the remains of an old wreck, sticking up out of the water. Some cormorants were resting on them.

"I wonder how old that is," said Theo. "Maybe it is a pirate's or smuggler's wreck! Let's see if we can reach it."

"Be careful. We have to watch the tide," answered Tyler. "Maybe we could just go a little way out."

The boys began to walk over the rocks, and Theo switched on the detector. They had got about halfway to the wreck when the machine began to buzz!

The two 'T's', as they were affectionately known, looked at each other in excitement. They only had beach spades with them, but they began to dig a hole. It was very frustrating because as they dug, the hole just kept filling up with sea water. Eventually Tyler gave a shout.

"I can see something quite big!" Theo looked into the hole, and then both boys abandoned their spades and dug with their hands, pulling out a rusty, decayed object.

"It looks like an old pistol!" said Theo excitedly. "That wreck must have been a pirates' ship or a smugglers'!"

The boys had been so busy digging the hole they hadn't realised how much the tide had come in until it began lapping around their feet.

"Goodness!" shouted Tyler. "We must run for the shore or we will be cut off by the tide!"

The boys began to feel frightened; they had to reach the other end of the cove where the cliff path would take them to safety. It wasn't easy trying to run over the rocks carrying spades, metal detector and the precious pistol. They were very breathless by the time they had scrambled up the cliff path that would lead them back to the cove where Tyler's dad was waiting. They sat down for a few moments to get their breath, and as they looked out to sea they realised what a narrow escape they had had!

"Dad might be getting worried. We must get back quickly!" remarked Tyler, so the two 'T's' began to walk along the cliff path back to Osmington. They had almost reached the cove when they passed the 'Smugglers' Inn'. Parts of the building were very old, but with new extensions it was still used as an inn.

"I wonder if our pistol belonged to someone who stayed at the inn?" said Theo, hugging the precious find to his chest. "I guess we have to tell someone official about our find. Perhaps we will learn its history."

They clambered down the cliff path to the beach where they had left Tyler's father. He was very glad to see the boys, for he was beginning to be concerned as they had been gone so long.

"Here you are!" he exclaimed. "I was thinking about sending out a rescue party to look for you!" Although he was joking, the boys could see he was worried.

"We're sorry, Dad," explained Tyler. "We did almost get cut off by the tide, but we were so excited because we found a pistol near the old wreck in the next bay. We think it must have belonged to a pirate or smuggler!"

The boys showed their find to Bill, and he whistled in surprise.

"Wow!" he said. "I think you may be right. However, we had better go home now, as you must be ready to start school tomorrow. Your mums will be cross if I am late getting you home! If you like, on Saturday I can take you to Dorchester museum and you can show the curator your pistol and maybe find out more about it and the wreck."

"Thank you," chorused the boys as they got into the car and began the journey home. What a fantastic last day of the holidays it had been!

Chapter Two

The next day Theo woke early. He was quite nervous about going to his new school, but excited too. His mum had laid out his new uniform, and he had already packed his backpack with his pens, pencils and other small items he thought he might need. He still had to add his lunch box. Today he didn't have to help his mother with the guests' breakfasts because it was such an important day. Only the year seven children who were new to the school were going today so that they would be able to find their way around the huge building and feel at home before term started properly the next day.

Theo ran down the hundred steps from his tower bedroom and into the kitchen. Mum was waiting with his breakfast and packed lunch. She gave him a hug, and he ran down the long drive to the entrance of the castle grounds where there were two stone pillars with carved lions on the top. Theo looked at them affectionately. They always reminded him of the Bible story of Daniel in the lions' den. He said a silent prayer to God that he would be as courageous as Daniel in this new school. He knew that it might be very hard to be a Christian in senior school.

A bus collected all the children who lived in the villages around Dorchester, so it made getting to school easy. When it arrived, Theo was glad to see Tyler was already on it and had saved him a seat. There were several other children from Much Syding School, and they all began to talk about the holidays. It was great to see everyone again! They stopped at Castle View Farm and collected Paul, who was a great friend of the two 'T's', and before they knew it they were at the school gates. A teacher was there to meet them, carrying a clipboard and pen to tick off their names and direct them to their form classrooms. Theo and Tyler had been praying that they would be in the same year group. Over the past few months, Theo had been helping Tyler with his literacy skills because he had missed so much schooling when his family were travelling the country in traditional Romany fashion. Much to their delight they, and Paul, were all in the same class. They found their classroom and were able to get desks near each other. Somehow it didn't seem so scary when your friends were near! It was confusing trying to find out where the different classrooms were for all the subjects. In the village school, there had only been three small rooms! Before lunch they had paid deposits and got locker keys and been told about timetables and registration. In fact, there was so much information their minds buzzed! The three boys went together to eat their packed lunch at a picnic table under a shady tree. Although it was September, it was still warm and sunny. The boys talked together.

"We must find out if there is a Christian group," suggested Paul. "We should start as we mean to go on, like our leader at Kidzone told us." The two 'T's' nodded, so they all three went to the main school notice board to see what clubs and groups there were.

"Look," said Theo, "there's something called a 'prayer space'. I wonder what that means?"

"I don't know," replied Paul, "but we can go and find out. I see there is a 'Faith is Fun' group too. Let's make a note of that. I want to go to the football trials. I'm sure you will go to the swimming ones, won't you, Theo?"

In fact there were so many groups, something to interest them all. They began to feel excited about their new school. There were so many new things they could do, including lots of sports and an environmental group that Tyler was excited to learn about. "I should probably join that too," Theo said. "The grounds of the castle are so big we ought to learn how to manage it. And for that matter, the river which runs through it too."

The afternoon went very quickly as the year seven children met different teachers, and it ended with the headmaster talking to them in assembly. He talked to them about the way he ran the school; what rules he insisted on; the zero bullying policy; the fact that wherever they went they would be representatives of the school. The boys went home very thoughtful but agreeing that being at senior school would be good.

The bus dropped Theo off at the castle gates. Tyler got off with him because it had been agreed that he and Theo could have a swim. The castle had its own pool in what used to be a large greenhouse, and the boys loved to use it! They walked up the long drive to the house and burst in through the kitchen door full of enthusiasm for the new school. Sally, Theo's mum, went to the fridge, found them some coke and cut some slices of cake. She was glad the day had gone so well.

"Do you have any homework to do before you swim?" she asked.

"We only have to write out our timetable," answered Theo.

"Well, do that first, and please make me a copy so that I know when you need sports gear, etc!" she answered.

The boys ran upstairs to the tower, getting quite out of breath as they did. "No wonder you keep fit, with all these stairs to climb!" commented Tyler.

"I know," answered Theo. "But it's worth it, having my own tower!" They wrote out the timetable as neatly as they could. Both boys wanted to do well at the new school. Then they listened to a CD of some of their favourite music before going down to have a swim. Theo got out the pistol they had found on the beach. He had wrapped it carefully in an old

14

towel. They admired it together and discussed taking it to the museum the following Saturday. It was very exciting!

As they left the tower and walked through the house, they could hear Penny, Theo's eldest sister, practising on the piano. She was going away to a boarding school in Manchester which specialised in music. They were all very proud of her because she had won a scholarship, and it looked as if her dream of becoming a concert pianist might come true. Theo knew he would miss Penny, and it would be very hard for his mother because she helped her so much with all the work that running a B&B entailed. However, Tyler's mum now came to the castle every morning to help while his gran looked after baby Sunshine, so everything was working out well! Theo sighed to himself. If only Dad hadn't left them and gone to live with another woman in Australia! Since he had become a Christian he had forgiven his dad, but sometimes it still made him feel sad

Chapter Three

The next few days were wet and windy, but school had begun in earnest, so it didn't worry the children too much. Theo's twin brother and sister, Sebastian and Felicity, usually known as Seb and Flick, were now in year nine and had lots of homework. They decided to join the school homework club, but Theo still went straight home on the bus so that he could help his mum when she had lots of guests.

In those first few days of school, Theo, Tyler and Paul all kept getting lost as they tried to get to the different classes on time! The new lessons were a bit baffling too. Straight away Tyler knew he would like Biology, but French was a nightmare for him as he still found reading and writing English hard.

One lunchtime they found the 'prayer space'. It was not much more than a big cupboard, but there were a few chairs and a board on which students and staff could write down their prayer requests. The boys found it was empty so they went in and the three of them decided to ask God to help them with all the new lessons. They wanted to do their best. As time went on they found this was a really special place for them, and they went there regularly to ask God for help and to thank him for answers too. One answer was the good idea that came to Theo that Tyler could go to his house after school each day and they would have their own 'homework club'. It was quiet in the tower, and they could help each other, whereas at Tyler's house his baby sister was often noisy. When they had done their homework, they were free to have a swim or to ride Tyler's gran's pony, which was stabled at the castle.

The first Saturday of term, Tyler's dad took them to Dorchester museum as he had promised. The pistol was still carefully wrapped up in a towel, and the boys proudly presented it to the curator. He examined it meticulously and told the excited boys that they had indeed found a pistol which could be about three hundred years old!

"Where did you find this?" he asked them.

"In the cove between Osmington Mills and Ringstead. We were using my metal detector near the remains of the old wreck," answered Theo. "Is it valuable?"

"Well," replied the curator, "it's not very valuable, but it is certainly very interesting. May I keep it for while and have it looked at and cleaned up? I will give you a receipt and phone you when it comes back."

The boys looked at each other and nodded. It would be good to find out a bit more about it. The curator asked the boys if they were interested in the history of the pirates and smugglers of the Dorset coast, and once again they nodded.

"Go to the exhibition on the second floor, and you will find out a lot," he said. "And you should visit Church Ope Cove on Portland. That is a very interesting place."

"Thank you so much for your help," said Tyler's dad, and they left their precious pistol in his care and went up to look at the exhibition. There was a lot to see and read about, and the boys were really interested. Bill had to drag them away because it was almost time to close the museum.

"I don't know about you two, but I want to hear the football results!" he said. The boys laughed because they knew that Bill supported a team which never did very well! They all hurried to the car park. Tyler's dad had never learnt to read or write because as a gypsy boy he spent most of his time travelling the country in a 'vardo'. Since Tyler had learnt to read, with Theo's help, he had been reading the Bible to his mother and father and also trying to help them to be able to read for themselves. Bill was finding it very hard, and on the way home from Dorchester he asked them to pray for him.

"Tyler was telling me about the prayer space you have in your new school," he said. "Please would you visit it and ask God to help me to be able to read."

"Of course we will, Dad," said Tyler, and Theo nodded in agreement. "We can ask for a miracle for you!"

They arrived back in the cottage in the woods where Tyler's family lived. Theo had been invited to stay for tea.

He always loved that because the family normally cooked and ate outside, and it was like a barbeque. Theo's gran lived in her own vardo, and the boys ran over to greet her. As usual she was sitting on the steps, and Sunshine was playing nearby. When the latter saw the boys, she toddled over to them. Tyler picked her up and swung her round, and she laughed and laughed!

After tea the boys told Gran all about their visit to the museum. She was very interested and said that her family used to camp on the island of Portland when she was a girl and that she loved to play in an old castle on the top of the cliff.

"It wasn't like the castle where you live, Theo," she added. "It was all ruins and quite dangerous, but we loved it! Portland is a great place to explore, but it isn't really an island, so the ponies could pull our vardo across. They struggled to get us up the hills though," she chuckled as she remembered. "We children had to all get out and walk, and even we got out of breath! We had no cars in those days!"

The boys decided they were definitely going to go to Portland and explore, even if they had to wait until the half term holiday.

Chapter Four

*N*ext week at school, the boys kept their promise and wrote down Tyler's father's prayer request. They asked God to perform a miracle because he so longed to read the Bible for himself. He did try very hard to learn to read, but with his job of taking care of the woods and looking after his family, he had so little time.

Theo, Tyler and Paul had also joined the 'Faith is Fun' group, abbreviated to 'Fif', which met in a lunch break each week. When their classmates found out, they were dubbed 'the God Squad' and laughed at for being 'sissies' by the other boys, but they tried to ignore the teasing because they did enjoy the group. Tyler shared at the group that his father needed prayer. When he told them the story of his parents becoming Christians because the words of a beautiful song had been 'given' to them one night, they were so interested, and all agreed they would pray for Bill. At the meeting they often read Bible passages together and discussed what they meant. They knew that it was so important for Christians to read God's word and try to obey it. The group was led by some year 10 students. One of them was going to be baptised very soon and invited everyone to come and support him if they could. Paul and the two 'T's' decided to ask their parents if they could go to the service.

Theo was very pleased one afternoon to see that he had done well in the swimming trials and had been given a place in the school junior squad. He had also joined the rugby club. He had loved playing rugby when he had been at prep school before his father had left home, but they hadn't played that game at Much Syding village school. He thought of how much he had hated the village school at first because he had been accused of being a 'snob' and the children were unfriendly. Then he thought of how he had met Tyler who also had had no friends and was bullied because he was a gypsy. Through his friendship with Tyler, he had come to learn about God and Jesus, and it had made such a difference to his life; then after an adventure, they had become friends with Paul and his brother and sister. So much had happened in the last six months! Theo put his hand into his blazer pocket and felt the bird whistle that Tyler had carved for his birthday and said a quiet 'Thank you' to God for his friend.

The castle didn't have many visitors now that the summer was over, so Theo and the twins were not needed to help so much. Penny had started at her boarding school and was happy, but Theo knew his mum worried a lot about having enough money. They all loved the castle and didn't want to have to sell it. Even their regular visitor, Mrs Samways, didn't come now that she had found her runaway son. Theo had always loved her visits. He thought perhaps he should go to the prayer space and put a request that they could stay at the castle.

One afternoon the two 'T's' got off the school bus and ran up the drive to find the kitchen full. Tyler's mum, gran and little Sunshine were having tea with Theo's mum, and they all seemed very excited.

"Hi, boys!" called out Theo's mum. "Come in and hear the news!"

"What's happened?" said Tyler, very surprised to see his family, especially his gran, in the kitchen sitting at the table.

"It's your dad," explained his mother. "Something amazing has happened to him!" She took a deep breath, then continued: "He came in for lunch and sat down. Your Bible was on the table and he picked it up and began to look at it! You know how hard it has been for him to try to read, as he hardly ever went to school. There are long and difficult words in the Bible too!

"Well, it was a miracle! Dad found he could read in a way that he had not managed before—and the words made sense. He could understand them! Dad became so excited! The more he read, the more he wanted to go on reading. I had a job to get him to eat his dinner and go back to work!"

The boys looked at each other in amazement! How could that have happened? It truly was a miracle! When they had prayed for a miracle they hadn't really expected anything to happen so quickly! Wow! Wait until the 'Fif' group at school hear this news! No wonder everyone was so excited! Tyler sat at the kitchen table and made his mum tell him about how it happened all over again. It was as if he couldn't take it in. His dad could read!

Suddenly, he got out his mobile. "I must text Paul," he said. Eventually he calmed down, and the boys had a drink and then decided to have a swim. Neither of them could concentrate on doing homework! Theo wondered if God would answer his prayer request in such an amazing way too. He was now very convinced that God did hear and answer prayer and that his prayer had been heard.

Tyler's dad was so excited about being able to read that he decided to take a week's holiday from work so that he could read more of the Bible for himself. He marvelled at what a wonderful book it was, especially when he read the gospels which tell the story of Jesus. The news of his miracle spread through the village, and some of the Christians came to thank God with him. This brought much happiness to the whole family since many of the village people had been suspicious of them, as they were of most gypsies. The minister of the church invited Bill to tell the congregation on the following Sunday about the miracle. He also wondered if both Bill and his wife would sing the song which had been given to them one night and started them thinking about Christianity.

That Sunday the church was packed! Of course, Theo
was there and so were his mum and the twins. It was a
very exciting service. When Bill and Betty sang 'The Song'
together, it was so beautiful that many people were wiping
their eyes. It seemed as if no one wanted to go home from
the service that morning, it had been such a special occasion.

The minister announced that the next weekend was to be
the Harvest festival. In the country this is a very important
thanksgiving, especially for the farmers. On the Saturday
evening, there was to be a harvest supper at the castle
followed by a barn dance in their barn. Theo was so pleased
about that. He didn't care about dancing, but a band
was coming, and also Tyler's parents were going to bring
their violins and play gypsy music. He thought it would
be great fun. Even his sister Penny was coming home for
the weekend, and although he hadn't told anyone, he was
missing his big sister, a lot.

Chapter Five

The week seemed to pass slowly for the boys. They tried to complete their homework quickly so that they would be free to help with all the preparations for the barn dance. One evening they were up in the tower room working when Theo's mum sent him a text. She often did that rather than climb the hundred steps to give him a message!

"A phone call for you, hurry downstairs," it said.

Theo dashed downstairs and Tyler followed him, not quite knowing what to do.

"Hello," said the caller. "This is the curator of Dorchester museum. Your pistol has been returned. Would you like to hear about it?"

"Oh yes, please!" replied Theo in excitement, and he pressed a button on the phone so that Tyler and his mother could hear what was said.

"Well," said the curator, "it has been dated to around 1830. It appears to be French in origin. Around that time there were French, Dutch and Spanish pirates as well as English smugglers operating around the Dorset coast line. The bays at Osmington and Ringstead were very popular because they were sheltered and also had paths that led up over the cliffs. There was one notorious smuggling family associated with Osmington, the leader of whom was a

man called Emmanuel Charles. He was born in January
of 1871, and by the time he was in his teens he was an
experienced smuggler. He brought brandy from France. In
1928 he was captured by the customs and excise men, and
the court sentenced him to serve in the navy. All his family
were involved in the illegal trade. As soon as he had served
his sentence, he returned to smuggling. It was a 'cat and
mouse' sort of game between the smugglers and the customs
officers, and they even had a sort of mutual respect for each
other!

"Eventually, he was captured in Cherbourg, France and
was brought back to England. In 1835 he was killed by a
pistol shot, fired by a coastguard off the Isle of Purbeck.
Of course, we don't know who owned your pistol, but it
could have been one of Emmanuel Charles's family as they
were all involved, including a relative by marriage, Ann
Clamp, who owned the 'Smugglers' Inn', as it is now called,
at Osmington Mills." The curator paused for a moment
to get his breath, and then continued: "Your pistol has
been registered as a find, and there is a possibility that the
archaeologists will investigate the area of the wreck in due
course. You are welcome to come back and collect the pistol.
Look after it well because although it is not terribly valuable,
it is interesting history!"

"Thank you so much, sir, for telling us all about it! We
will come and collect it very soon, perhaps even tomorrow

after school." Theo looked at his mum, and she nodded in agreement.

Tyler and Theo were so excited about the news. They discussed what to do with the pistol since it really belonged to both of them. As they were discussing this, the twins came in from school after their homework club. They joined in the discussion, and Seb came up with the idea that for six months of the year it could be on display in the castle and the other six months it could be kept in the vardo which belonged to Tyler's gran. Tyler didn't want it in Honeysuckle Cottage where he lived, as his sister Sunshine was still just a toddler and could get hold of it and damage it. It seemed a sensible solution, and before Tyler went home they also agreed not to come home on the school bus the next day but that Theo's mum would meet them at the museum.

When they collected the pistol, they found it had been carefully cleaned and looked much nicer. It had been put into a box with a glass lid so that it could be displayed, and there was a printed certificate to say where it had been found and its approximate age. The boys were so delighted with it and carried their treasure home with many thanks to the curator.

"We haven't forgotten about visiting Church Ope Cove in Portland, either," said Tyler as they were saying goodbye. "We hope to go there in the half term if the weather is fine."

"Good," replied the curator. "It's the best way to learn history, exploring places yourselves. I don't think you will ever forget about the French pirates and the Dorset smugglers!"

On Friday evening, Penny came home for the weekend, and Theo was so happy to see her again. He hadn't realised he would miss his big sister so much! He even missed hearing her piano practice. It was really nice being a whole family again, or almost whole, because Theo longed to see his dad once more. He had accepted that it might not happen as Australia was so far away and his dad now had a new family. He heard that he now had a stepsister, and he wished he could see her. He wondered if she would be as cute as Sunshine, who made everybody laugh! Her name was Lucy Jane and she was only two months old.

All the family helped their mother to get the castle ready for the Harvest supper and barn dance. The boys had to sweep the barn. It needed it! Theo looked after the chickens and ducks, and sometimes they found their way into the barn. As they were cleaning, he found a few old eggs which needed to be thrown away. Paul's father had provided some bales of hay, which they then placed around the walls of the barn for people to sit on. There were folding chairs for the musicians and a few other chairs for older people to sit on. They decorated the barn with coloured leaves and branches with hawthorn berries. When they had finished, it looked really good. Inside the castle, the girls had been decorating the large dining room with flowers and autumn leaves. Theo had asked his mum if he could invite some of his school friends both from his year group and also from the 'Fif' group. She was very happy for them to come, and Seb and Flick also asked some of their schoolmates.

Saturday was a crisp and sunny autumn day, and everyone was glad it was fine. Lots of the women from the church brought food. It looked as if it would be a fantastic meal! As well as the barn dance, the youth club leader had organised a sort of treasure hunt in the grounds and a table tennis tournament because he guessed the boys probably didn't want to dance. It ended up being a fantastic party which everyone seemed to enjoy very much. At the end of the meal, the minister reminded everyone how good God is in providing the harvest year by year, and they all joined in a song of thanks. The school friends seemed to enjoy themselves. One of their classmates remarked to them that they didn't realise that church events could be fun. Some of them had been shown the pistol and heard all about the pirates and smugglers. They were also green with envy when they learnt that Theo had a room in the tower, even if he did have to climb a hundred stairs to reach it!

Lying in bed that night, Theo thought how much his life had changed in the past year. From being so sad and lonely, he now had many friends and one very special friend, Tyler. Both of them had become Christians and so knew Jesus, the very best friend of all! He quietly whispered "thank you" as he dozed off to sleep.

Chapter Six

One day soon after the barn dance, the boys were down in the woods looking for animal tracks when they were disturbed by the sound of a helicopter. It was very low and seemed as if it would get caught in the trees. It kept hovering round and round, and they wondered what was going on. They were used to air-sea rescue helicopters, but those just flew over to the coast. Eventually, it flew away, so the boys forgot about it and continued to look for badger scratching posts and also to watch the squirrels collecting acorns for the winter. Tyler knew so much about wildlife. He was never happier than when he was roaming in the woods. He knew every inch of them and loved to watch the changing seasons. Just now the autumn leaves were beginning to fall, and it seemed to Tyler that it was like a soft blanket wrapping up the ground and all the little creatures ready to sleep until spring.

Tyler had been teaching Theo how to recognise bird songs, and they began to practise the sounds. It was like having a secret language of their own. Sometimes Tyler also taught his friend the Romany words for birds and animals. Although his family no longer roamed around the country, they were still fiercely proud of their heritage and wanted to preserve their customs and language. The family were so much happier now that they were accepted in the community of Much and Little Syding. No longer were they the first suspects if there was any trouble in the area.

The boys sat down on a tree stump and chatted. "Do you remember how we found Sam, the tramp?" said Tyler.

"Yeah, I'll never forget that adventure!" replied Theo. "It was so fantastic to find he was Mrs Samways's long lost son! By the way, she is coming down to stay with us in a couple of weeks," he added.

"Is Sam coming too, and how about his dog, Laddie?" asked Tyler.

"Mum didn't say anything about them, but I'll ask her," said Theo. "Anyway, I'm really glad Mrs Samways is coming because mum needs some more guests. We don't get many at this time of year, and Mrs Samways is such a lovely old lady, and I like talking to her."

As they chatted, they heard the noise of the helicopter again, this time not quite so close.

"I wonder what is going on?" queried Tyler. "Maybe the police are chasing someone. Let's go to the clearing and see if we can see the 'copter."

The boys chased over to the edge of the woods where they could see the sky.

"I'm not quite sure what the writing says on it," said Theo. "It's the wrong colour for police or air-sea rescue. Perhaps someone's just having lessons!"

"No, look! I can see now," exclaimed Tyler. "It's the Environment Agency. I wonder what they are looking at. Maybe it's the woods, but there are no dangers of forest fires now. I must ask dad if he knows." Tyler paused for breath and then added, "Let's go to my house. I'm starving, and I promised Gran I'd collect some kindling this morning for the fire."

The boys started to walk in the direction of Honeysuckle Cottage, gathering small twigs as they went. By the time they reached Tyler's home, they had their arms full. They went first to the beautifully painted gypsy vardo at the back of the cottage, where Gran still liked to live. It was her pride and joy. Inside was so compact and neat. All her treasures were displayed in a glass fronted cabinet fixed on the back wall. Among the treasures she had made a space to display the smuggler's pistol when it was Tyler's turn to have it.

"We've brought the kindling, Gran!" Tyler shouted to his grandmother, who was now quite deaf.

"Thank you boys. Come and have some scones and hot chocolate. I've just finished baking them," she answered.

The two 'T's' didn't need a second invitation! They washed their hands under the tap outside the cottage and climbed up the ladder into the vardo. It was so cosy inside! After they had eaten, Gran asked them about their morning, what they had seen and done. They talked about all the signs of autumn in the woods, and she told them about looking for mushrooms and how to recognise which ones were good to eat. Then she told them how the hedgehogs hibernated and how, when she was a child, they used to dig them out from under the piles of leaves. She explained to them that they were a delicacy when baked in mud in the ashes of the fire. When the mud case was removed all the prickly spines fell off, leaving very tender meat that tasted even better than chicken.

"Now, of course, meat is not scarce and we no longer cook hedgehogs. Indeed, there are not so many around. They say it is due to all the slug and snail pellets that people use in their gardens. These not only deprive the hedgehogs of their source of food, for they love to eat garden pests, but can also make hedgehogs ill if they eat poisoned pests."

They boys loved being with Gran. She had so many stories of the 'old days' when the gypsies roamed around the country, living off the land.

"Now boys," she said, when her stories had stopped. "I am tired and need to rest, but I do want some blackberries. Can you get me some?" She produced two little woven baskets and sent the boys off hunting.

"By the way," she added, looking at Theo, "how's my pony Sparky doing?"

"He's fine, Gran," answered Theo. "Flick grooms and rides him every day, and we all love him. Would you like me to ride him over to see you soon?"

"That would be lovely," Gran said, "I know he is happy in your paddock and stable, but I do miss my faithful mate. He has drawn this vardo all over this country!"

The boys left Gran to have a nap and went out into the lanes to pick blackberries. It was a good year for them, and they picked (and ate!) masses. Soon their baskets were full. On the way home, they noticed a patch of mushrooms. Theo found a bag in his backpack, and they picked those too. They were pretty sure they were mushrooms and not toadstools but knew that Gran would check them. On their way back, walking along the river bank, the boys became very excited because they saw two otters playing! It was the first time that Theo had seen otters, and he was entranced. They were so sleek and skilful as they swam in the river. The boys stayed and watched, hardly daring to move a muscle in case they frightened them away! They had talked at school in biology about otters returning to the rivers in the west country, now that pollution was less. To actually see them was fantastic, and they thought they should tell the biology mistress they had done so.

The afternoon passed so quickly, and it began to get cool. They hurriedly picked up their baskets and ran back to the vardo where Gran was waiting. She had lit the outside fire and was cooking a stew for the evening meal. When she saw the blackberries and mushrooms, she was delighted. "I'll make some blackberry jelly, and you can have a pot for your mum," she told Theo. "Anyway, I hope you are staying for supper! There is plenty of stew for us all!"

Tyler's mum walked over. "Why don't we ring your mother and see if you can have a sleepover?" she asked. "It's a nice evening, and we can eat outside and sing around the camp fire! We can all go to church in the morning, and you can go home from there."

"Oh yes, please!" answered Theo, delighted. As it was the weekend, his mum didn't mind at all. The supper tasted wonderful. After they had eaten, they all toasted marshmallows in the fire for a treat. Tyler's parents brought out their instruments, and everyone sang folk songs and then some Christian ones. Bill proudly got his Bible and read to them all without any mistakes or hesitation. He read the whole story of Ruth from the Old Testament. It was a wonderful story, and Theo was not sure if he had ever heard it before. He thought it was amazing that Ruth chose to become one of God's people and that even though she was an immigrant to Israel, she became an ancestor of Jesus. Bill explained that he had read it because it was a harvest time story and how thankful they all were for the good harvest. Before they all went to bed, they thanked God for the harvest, and Theo added his own thanks for the blackberries and mushrooms and also that they had seen the beautiful otters in the river.

Chapter Seven

The next day, when Theo was walking home from church, telling his mum all about the things he and Tyler had been doing the day before, he suddenly remembered the helicopter.

"I heard and saw it too," his mum replied. "In fact it kept circling over the castle grounds for a long time. Maybe it is some kind of survey. If it is anything important, we shall hear in due course, I'm sure."

"One more week of school, and then it is half term!" Theo said happily to his mum. "Tyler and I want to go to Portland and explore the Church Ope Cove as the curator of the museum suggested."

"Sounds a nice idea. We'll work out the transport for you. It's too far to cycle from here. Let's hope the weather stays good for you. I shall be busy because we have some people booked in to stay, including Mrs Samways. She will be pleased to see you!" answered his mother.

"Is Sam coming too, and Laddie?" asked Theo.

"I don't think so; she has just booked one bedroom. I guess she'll tell you all the news when she sees you. Penny will be home to help me, and Tyler's mum is going to give me a hand too, so you and the twins will be free most of the time."

Although the two 'T's' loved their new school, they were both looking forward to the holiday. They had been planning to do quite a lot of things together. The last day of the holiday was when their school friend was going to be baptised, and they were looking forward to being at the service and encouraging him. At school they were still laughed at for being part of 'the God Squad', but they had got used to it and found the group very friendly. The meetings had taught them a lot about being Christians and getting to know Jesus better. Theo had been baptised as a baby, but Tyler had not, and so they both wanted to know what being baptised as a believer meant.

Mrs Samways arrived on the first weekend of the holiday. She looked so bright and happy that Theo thought she must have grown younger, not older! She was so pleased to see him and wanted to hear all about senior school. They walked around the castle grounds together catching up on each other's news. It was amazing how you could be a friend of someone as old as your grandmother!

"How's Sam?" asked Theo.

"He's fine! Thank you," replied Mrs Samways. "He has now got a job! That's so amazing after all these years and having so little education. He works at a care home and is wonderful at looking after the elderly folk there. He has moved out from my wee house and lives in a flat of his own. It is quite near, so I see a lot of him. I never thought he would settle down having been a tramp for so many years, but he seems happy, and we are both enjoying life again! Laddie is quite an old dog, and I take him for walks when Sam is at work. He is good company for me. I can never thank you enough for finding my runaway son for me!"

"That was quite an adventure finding him, wasn't it!" remarked Theo. "Tyler and I have had another adventure since then." He proceeded to tell his friend all about the pirate pistol. "We are going to Portland one day next week to explore another cove known for smuggling and piracy," he added.

The Monday of half term was a bright day, but everyone was too busy to take the two 'T's' to Portland, so Theo decided it was a good day to ride Sparks, the pony, over to see Gran. Flick loved Sparks and was the one who really took care of him. His coat gleamed from all her grooming! He was not a young pony and trotted sedately along the road from Little Syding to Much Syding. They took a short cut through the woods and were soon at Honeysuckle Cottage. Tyler was waiting for him, and they went straight over to Gran's vardo. She was so thrilled to see her pony again, and he muzzled against her. The boys left her and went to the river to see if the otters were playing. They also fished for crayfish and were delighted to catch quite a few.

"Gran will be pleased with these!" exclaimed Tyler. "She'll cook them for her supper!" When they took them to her, she was indeed delighted. As she had promised, she gave Theo a pot of bramble jelly which she had made from the blackberries they had picked for her a week or so earlier. He knew his mum would love it!

The boys loved being with Gran. She had so many stories about the time when the Romany gypsies travelled up and down the country. That morning she taught them how to make 'dolly' clothes pegs, even though they were not sold from door to door any more. It was the first time that Theo had carved anything, and Gran was very careful that he used the knife in the correct way. He found it quite hard, but was so pleased with the results!

As the boys worked, Gran told them wonderful stories about potato picking in the Fenlands, strawberry picking in Somerset and big family gatherings at fairs.

"Do you miss it, Gran?" asked Tyler.

"I find it hard to stay in one place, although I love living here with you all. I realise that I lived in a lot of fear and superstition. The most wonderful thing of all is to have learnt about Jesus and know the peace he gives!" she answered. "I am an old lady and have had a wonderful life, but I wish I had known Jesus as my friend when I was young. 'The Song' which was given to Bill and Betty was the most wonderful thing that ever happened to our family! Before I knew Jesus I didn't know that fortune-telling was wrong. Now I know that only Jesus really knows the future,

and we must trust him to give us what is the best for us. I
had no idea that there was a plan for our lives. I'm glad you
two haven't had to wait until you are as old as I am to learn
about these things!"

The day seemed to pass very quickly, and soon Sparky was
trotting back along the road to the castle. Tyler's dad had
promised to drive the boys to Portland the next morning
if the weather was fine, so Theo had arranged to be ready
with his picnic and metal detector as soon as he had finished
helping his mum with breakfasts.

The next day was cold but sunny. Theo was up early
and helped his mum as he had promised. Then he fed his
chickens and ducks. As soon as he had finished, he sent a
text to Tyler, made himself a packed lunch and got his gear
together for the expedition. He put his metal detector into
his backpack. It stuck out of the end, but that was OK.
Then he decided he might need a pencil and note pad, his
camera, a small towel in case they paddled in rock pools and
his mobile phone. He added his lunch, a bar of chocolate
and a bottle of water and then closed his backpack. Then
he had a second thought; it seemed silly, but perhaps he
would need a penknife and a torch, so he quickly added
these. Then, after saying goodbye to his mum, he ran down
the drive to wait at the entrance of the castle for Bill to pick
him up. A few minutes later, he saw the car and climbed in

alongside Tyler. Both boys felt really excited. They also felt quite grown up because they were having this adventure on their own. Bill took them to the car park for Church Ope Cove and told them to cross the road carefully. He was going to do some business in Weymouth and then Abbotsbury and expected to pick them up about 3.30pm. He told the boys to phone him if they were worried or needed him to come before then and warned them only to paddle in the shallow water.

The boys waved to Bill and crossed the road carefully. It was easy to find the lane which led down to the cove. After a few yards, they saw the remains of Rufus Castle standing high above them. Because it was a ruin and so near the edge of the cliff, it was enclosed by iron railings and no longer open to the public to explore. Tyler in particular was sad about this because he remembered that his gran had played there in her youth. However, it did look magnificent, and Theo was glad he had brought his camera with him and could take some photos. Tyler had learnt from his gran, who had a marvellous memory, that the castle used to be called 'Bow and Arrow' Castle and was built about 900 years ago. Additional fortifications had been added in 1238 by Richard de Clare. Theo was sorry that he wasn't able to go around the grounds with the metal detector. Who knows what they might have found! From the castle the lane became just a little track, and it wound very steeply down into Church Ope Cove itself. The cove was quite small and well protected. The boys could imagine how good it would have been for smugglers to land their small boats. There was still a rusty winch for hauling boats up on to the shore. They couldn't see any boats, not even fishing or rowing boats, but there were many small beach huts. Most of them were surrounded by low walls made of large pebbles and were all higgledy-piggledy under the cliffs. On that October day, they appeared to be deserted and locked up. As the boys explored, they noticed one had had the lock broken, and they pushed the door and peered inside. It was empty, just like a shed, and it smelt dank. They left the beach huts and strolled down to the water's edge, over the pebbly beach. The water was very clear, and when they took off their shoes and socks to paddle, they were really surprised at how warm it was. Soon they were splashing around and having lots of fun. They looked for marine life but only saw a few shrimps and tiny crabs. The boys thought how nice it would be to swim in the summer as the cove was so sheltered.

As they were drying their feet, Theo got out his bar of chocolate and, dividing it in half, gave some to Tyler. They sat and munched, enjoying the autumn sunshine.

"Gran told me a funny story about this cove," said Tyler. "I wonder if it could really be true! She said in the 19th century a camel's carcass was washed up on the shore! The local people were so scared and had never seen a camel. They thought it was a monster!"

"Wherever would a camel have come from?" asked Theo.

"I have no idea! That is why I wonder if it is just a tale or a real story!" answered Tyler. "Did you notice at the top of the lane was a small museum? Dad told me it's not often open in the winter, but in the summer we could come and find out more about this place. I think it would be a nice place for a family picnic for us all!"

"Yes, but what a steep path to carry Sunshine's buggy down!" laughed Theo.

For a while the boys sat watching the gulls and then decided to do more exploring before they ate their lunch. They noticed another steep path that went up the cliff, and it had a signpost to the church ruins and Pennsylvania Castle.

"Another castle!" exclaimed Theo, "I didn't know there were two castles here, also a ruined church. Maybe that's why it is called 'Church Ope Cove'."

The boys climbed the path, getting quite out of breath as it was so steep. Suddenly they came to a level part where there were ruins. They saw an area where once a church had stood. There was still a pointed archway, but now it was covered in ivy. There was also an area with old grave stones. There were no walls left in the church, but the boys could see where they must have been. It was all slightly eerie but interesting. Theo got out his metal detector and began to walk over the church floor area. Meanwhile Tyler began to look at the grave stones. Some were so old that he couldn't read the engraving on them, others had fallen over and were overgrown with grass and weeds. One interested him very much because it had a skull and crossbones engraved on it.

"Come and see this stone," he called to Theo, who put down the metal detector and ran over.

"Do you think it belonged to a pirate?" he asked. "I think it could have. Look, I can just make out the date … 1798 … I'm sure that's the time the pirates from France, Spain and Holland were terrorising the Dorset coast as well as the smugglers working here."

The boys were examining the grave, and then while Theo sat on it for a moment, there was a scrunching sound, and to their horror and amazement the top of the grave began to swing to one side, revealing steps down to a tunnel. The boys looked at each other.

"Shall we … dare we?" said Tyler, and after a moment's hesitation, Theo nodded.

Chapter Eight

The boys were scared, but also excited. Theo was shivering as he climbed down into the grave. He was scared that there might be a skeleton and for some reason found himself whispering to Tyler.

"Let's just have a quick look, and then we can come back into the sunshine and eat our lunch. Maybe it was a secret place where the smugglers stored their contraband and an escape route for the pirates and not a grave at all."

It was dark inside the tunnel, and suddenly Theo remembered the torch. What a good job he had put it in! He fumbled around his back pack and located it. Both of the boys felt better when the light was shining! They reached the bottom step and as they did so, they heard the scrunching sound again and looked up to see the top of the grave closing over them. Then they really panicked! "How are we going to get out?" whispered Tyler in great fear.

"I don't know." Theo was almost panicking. Then he stopped and turned to Tyler. "There must be a way out. The pirates or whoever made this tunnel either had some way of opening it again when the danger had passed or it lead them somewhere safe. Ty, we must pray for help. I seem to remember that we learnt a verse that said, 'When I am afraid, I will trust in you.' We need to do that now."

The boys were crouching in the tunnel—it was too small to stand up straight—but they stopped and asked God to help them and lead them to safety. Theo flashed the torch around to see if he could find any device that might open the grave stone again, but there didn't seem to be any.

"I think we should go on and see where it leads," he said, trying to be very grown up and keeping calm, but really he felt like crying. So the boys slowly crept along the tunnel, and eventually it lead into quite a big cavern. As they entered the cavern, they heard a noise and almost jumped out of their skins! Someone spoke to them! They heard a weak voice call, "Help." Theo flashed his torch around the cavern and saw a man lying on the ground. Cautiously they walked over to him, glad to be able to stand upright at last, but also very frightened.

"Who are you?" Tyler asked the man. He was looking very ill and was trying to move.

"I am hurt. I think my leg is broken," he whispered with long pauses between his sentences because he was so weak. "Have you any water? I have been here five days."

Theo quickly undid his backpack and found his water and held it to the man's mouth.

"Sip it slowly," he told him, remembering hearing someone say that a starving person should eat and drink very slowly. When the man had had a small amount to drink, Tyler asked him if he could manage to eat and produced one of his sandwiches. The man grabbed it quickly—he was obviously very hungry. So the boys each shared some food with him and were about to eat some themselves when Tyler decided, "We had better ration this out, in case we're not rescued for a while."

Theo nodded, and the real nature of their predicament hit him again. He felt for his mobile. He should have thought of doing it before.

"I'll try to phone Mum," he said. When he got out his phone, the man's face darkened a bit, and he looked frightened.

Theo tried to phone and to text, but there was no signal. There was nothing he could do. What should they do next? He looked at Tyler and could see he was frightened too. He said out loud to himself, "When I am afraid, I will trust in you. Oh Jesus, I need your help now!" he cried. Then he flashed his torch around the cavern and saw that there seemed to be an exit on the other side.

"Ty, one of us has to go on and try to find where this tunnel comes out," he said. "Or should we both go and then bring someone back to help this man?"

The man had been listening to the boys. He tried to lift up his head. "Please don't leave me!" he begged them.

It was a really hard decision to make. Only one could have the torch, and that really needed to be the person going through the tunnel. The man wasn't really a threat to them, though they had both guessed who he might be. They had heard on the local news several days ago that a prisoner had escaped from the Verne prison on Portland. The police had searched the area and given up the chase when there was no trace of him, guessing he would be miles away.

"One of us has to go," Theo told the prisoner. "We know who you are and that you escaped from the prison. We have to get help or we will all die here." He shuddered at the thought. "I will go on," he suddenly and decisively said, "if that's alright with you, Tyler. I'm sorry I shall have to leave you in the dark. I'll leave my backpack with you. I'll be as quick as I can." Tyler nodded, not happy, but knowing a decision had to be made.

"Thank you," whispered the prisoner. "I've been so frightened, and I thought I would just die in this cave. It's like a miracle that you boys have come. I won't hurt you."

Tyler sat on the floor near the prisoner and reached out and held his hand. He smelt pretty awful having been there for five days, unable to move, but Tyler felt a wave of pity for the man. Even that helped him to forget his own terror a bit. As he sat in the darkness he began to sing 'The Song' that had changed his family life. Tyler loved to sing, and the sweet music about Jesus filled the cavern. His voice seemed to swell as if there were a whole choir singing, and the prisoner began to cry.

Gradually the terror that Tyler had been feeling began to seep away, and he felt peaceful. He just knew at that moment that Jesus was in the cavern with him. Knowing that made him sing even more loudly, so much so that Theo could hear the distant echo as he slowly made his way through the tunnel. It had obviously not been used for many, many years, and in places earth had fallen, partly blocking the way. He went gently, praying he would be able to get through and there would be no further earth falls. The distant sound of 'The Song' gave him courage. Suddenly he saw a tiny bit of light, and his heart leapt! He must be near the exit of the tunnel! He tried to hurry, but it was getting a bit damp and slippery. Gradually he got nearer the light and was even able to switch off the torch. The exit was hidden by a hedge of ivy and brambles. How different those brambles seemed compared with the ones where they had picked blackberries for Gran just a few days ago! He pushed his way through them, having nothing but his bare hands to pull them away. He was very scratched and bleeding, but so thankful to get out of the tunnel. But where was he? Theo looked around him, confused both by the light and also that he seemed to be in an odd place. It was almost like a dry swimming pool, but it was very old. He realised he would have to climb out of it somehow and find his way to somewhere to get help.

Once his eyes had adjusted to the light, Theo looked at his watch. It was 3.30pm. Tyler's dad would be waiting for them. He reached into his pocket for his mobile, then realised in dismay that he had left it back in the cavern in his backpack. How stupid! He was so cross with himself he felt like bursting into tears! Then he thought he must climb out of this strange structure and go and get help.

"Help me, Lord," he whispered out loud, for after all the shock and fear he felt wobbly and weak. He began to look around for the best place to climb and eventually found there were a few hidden steps, very broken, but still able to be climbed. Once out, again he looked around to get his bearings and saw a little path. He followed it and found it led up a hill and through some woods. Suddenly, he saw a castle! It wasn't a ruin like Rufus Castle but looked very posh, like a hotel. It must be the other castle that Tyler had told him about. Theo began to run towards it, taking no notice of the sign warning that trespassers would be prosecuted and to beware of the dogs. All he wanted was to get help!

When he rang the bell a lady opened the door and looked at Theo with horror. Afterwards he realised what a sight he must have looked, having groped his way through the tunnel and been scratched by so many brambles! However, she listened as he tried to tell his story and bless her, she did believe him, even though it must have seemed very far-fetched talking about smugglers and prisoners and tunnels from graves. The first thing she did was to phone the police and tell them the story. Then she allowed Theo to phone his mother.

"Thank goodness you are alright. I have just had Bill on the phone saying he has searched for you boys everywhere and all he found was your metal detector in an old graveyard. What has happened?" Theo tried to explain again, and his mum promised to phone Bill back at once.

Theo wanted to go straight back to the cavern, but the owner of Pennsylvania Castle insisted that the best thing to do was to wait for the police to arrive. Meanwhile she made Theo a mug of hot chocolate and some ham sandwiches. He hadn't realised how cold and hungry he was! She found a rug and wrapped him in it. Eventually the shock began to wear off, and he stopped shaking.

Chapter Nine

Meanwhile, back in the cavern, Tyler was becoming accustomed to the dark. He realised the prisoner was listening to his singing, so he racked his brain to think of more songs he could sing. He remembered when he was small his Gran used to sing him Romany songs. They were jolly, and he used to dance and clap in time to them. He tried hard to remember the words, and as he sang the prisoner began to smile a little. He was very weak, and every time he moved he winced with pain.

"You are Roma?" he whispered in his weak voice. "Me too, Roma, from Bulgaria."

"I am a Romany Gypsy," answered Tyler, "but now we live in a house. Gran still lives in her vardo but no longer travels. Where is Bulgaria?"

"Far away in Eastern Europe and very cold. Everyone despises us Roma people." The prisoner began to cough, and Tyler brought out the water bottle again, hoping it might help. The man grabbed it and began to gulp it down, and Tyler was alarmed and concerned he might make himself sick. He firmly said 'no' and took the bottle away. "We might be here for a long time, and we need to ration the water," he said. He found another sandwich, and they shared it. "Eat it slowly, so that you get used to eating again," he advised.

It seemed ages since Theo had left them, and Tyler wondered how he was getting on. He must have found a way out, he thought to himself, otherwise surely he would have come back by now … unless … and the awful thought came to him … he has also hurt himself and is lying injured somewhere! Tyler began to shiver as he worried about his friend. Then he remembered the verse Theo had quoted: "When I am afraid I will trust in you."

"Lord, please help us. Help me not to be afraid and to trust you. Amen," he whispered quietly.

The feeling of terror went away, and he began to sing again. It helped the time to go more quickly. At least Tyler felt it did. In reality he had no idea what the time was. It almost seemed days since they had sat on the gravestone and it moved, revealing the tunnel. Thinking about that, Tyler remembered that Theo had left his metal detector behind when they climbed into the grave! "Wow," he thought, "my dad will look for us, and surely he will find it and realise we must be near!" The thought encouraged him a lot. Thinking of his dad made him sing 'The Song' again. The music filled the cavern, and Tyler felt he and the prisoner were safe. It was almost as if angels were in the cavern too. The prisoner squeezed his hand. "Beautiful song," he said.

"I'll tell you about it," said Tyler, "It's the song which changed our family. We stopped being travelling Romanies and mum stopped telling fortunes after they were given that song one night."

Tyler began to tell the prisoner all about how his parents woke up one night with the words and music of 'The Song' in their heads. Both of them, at the same time! The song had been given to them by God, they know that now, but then they had no idea what the words meant. Tyler went on to explain how 'The Song' had led them to meet some Christian Romanies, and their family had become Christians too. He told the prisoner so many things. It was easy to talk to someone in the dark. He even told him how confused and angry he had felt when they first stopped travelling. He had hated school, and everyone bullied him because he was a gypsy who couldn't even read. He told him how, as a gypsy family, they were blamed for everything that went wrong in the village and also how even their Romany relatives despised them because they were Christians. Then he told him about Theo, who was also bullied because he lived in a castle and had been to a 'posh' school, and how they had become best friends. Now the families were great friends, and they also had lots of friends in the village. "And it's all because of 'The Song'," he ended.

"Sing it again," begged the prisoner. So Tyler began to sing once more, until he heard someone call his name!

He stopped and shouted at the top of his voice, "We're here! Help us!"

Chapter Ten

*A*fter the phone call to his mother, everything seemed to happen very quickly. First the police arrived; Theo could hear their arrival by the noise of the sirens! Then Bill was at the door, carrying his metal detector and wanting to know where Tyler was and what was happening! The next on the scene were the paramedics and, soon after, the fire brigade! The lady who lived at Pennsylvania Castle was vey calm and told the assembled crews the story. She told them about John Penn's bathing pool which had been carved out of the rock about 200 years previously, now almost hidden because it was such a ruin and covered in brambles.

"I had no idea there was a tunnel leading from there to the 'pirate's tomb', which is what we have always called the grave with the skull and crossbones carved on the headstone," she explained, "or that that tomb was a secret passage either. I am not surprised though, because there is a history of piracy and smuggling all along this part of the coast."

"Well, we must get a rescue operation underway at once," said the police sergeant. "We may need all three emergency services. It will be getting dark soon, and we must get your lad out and also our escaped prisoner. It's a wonder he is still alive after five days underground with a broken leg."

One paramedic stayed to look after Theo, who was very indignant that he wasn't allowed to go with the rescue team! His scratches were cleaned, he was checked over to see that he was not injured and then the kind lady made tea for them both. Theo told her how he and his family lived in the castle at Little Syding. He also told her about how they had to run a bed and breakfast business in order to afford to stay there. She seemed to understand completely.

Then the lady told Theo about her castle. It was called Pennsylvania Castle because it had been built by John Penn, a grandson of the founder of Pennsylvania State in the U.S.A. John Penn had been a friend of King George III, who had given him the land. In 1800 the king and queen had come to visit him in the castle!

"Of course, King George III was a frequent visitor to Weymouth, and his visits made it the popular resort it is today!" she added. Her storytelling took Theo's mind off the rescue a little, and he was surprised when the phone rang and he heard the sergeant ask her if she would mind putting on the kettle once again!

"Good news," she announced to Theo and the paramedic. "The rescue is going well, and I will soon have some more visitors for tea! This has been the most exciting day I have had for years! It can be very boring living alone in a big castle with only dogs for company!"

"You must come and visit us in our castle," replied Theo, "It's never boring, especially when we have lots of guests or the church is having an event in the grounds or barn!"

The rescue was going well. The police, medics and firemen had split into two teams: one group tackling the entrance through the grave stone and the other group through the bathing pool. One of the men sat on the grave all the time, so that it would not swing back and trap the men. Both teams had to take great care as they made their way through the old tunnels, in case they collapsed. They rigged up good lighting as they went along, and this revealed places in the passageways which were particularly unsafe. The firemen shored these up with props. The team who entered by the grave stone were the first to reach Tyler and the prisoner. Both the man and the boy were dazzled by the bright lights as the rescue squad arrived. Once Tyler could focus again, he saw his dad was with the men, and he gave a 'whoop' of delight! His dad was equally happy to see his son safe and well.

The prisoner looked scared, but he was in so much pain and so weak all that mattered was to get him out of the cavern and to the hospital. He still clung on to Tyler's hand repeating, 'Roma, Roma, Roma' in his weak voice. Tyler explained to his dad and the rescuers that he was a Romany gypsy from Bulgaria. Bill knelt down beside the man and tried to reassure him in the Romany language that he was being rescued and would be taken to hospital. He seemed to understand.

"I need to take my son, Tyler, through the passage and back to his friend," Bill explained. "But do not be afraid. If I am allowed I shall come to visit you in the hospital." Reluctantly the prisoner let go of Tyler's hand, and his father began to lead him down the passage and to safety. It was dark when they climbed out of the grave, but the fireman who was sitting on the stone had a spare torch and showed them the path to the castle. Even though Tyler was eleven, he was glad to hold Dad's hand as they climbed the path. At the castle they were greeted by Theo, and once the paramedic had checked him over, Tyler too was treated to hot chocolate and a mountain of sandwiches. He was starving, having only eaten half a sandwich all day! Then, while they waited to hear news of the rescue team, they listened to Tyler's story of his time with the prisoner.

Getting through the tunnel was much more difficult for the prisoner. The paramedics had put his broken leg into a splint and given him a gas and air mixture through a mask to try and ease the pain. Since he was very weak, they were not able to give him as many pain-killing drugs as they would have liked, so the journey to the surface was pretty uncomfortable. He was strapped onto a stretcher, but there was very little room to move it through the tunnel. Inch by inch the men eased him back to the opening of the grave and lifted him out. As an escaped convict, he should have been handcuffed to one of the policemen but, as they so aptly remarked, there was no way he could escape now he was strapped down and very weak with a broken leg! Everyone concerned was just so thankful that they had managed the rescue without the passageways falling in, and they proceeded to lift the prisoner and climb the steep path that led to the main road where the ambulance was waiting. Once he was safely installed in the ambulance, he was driven off to Dorchester Hospital with a police escort. Those of the team who were left went back to Pennsylvania Castle to tell the folk waiting there that the rescue had been successful. They cheered and congratulated the men, and more drinks and sandwiches miraculously appeared from the kitchen!

The police sergeant wanted to talk to the boys, but seeing how tired they were, he suggested that he visit them the next morning to get their full story. The two 'T's' nodded in agreement. When Bill asked the officer if he would be allowed to visit the prisoner in the hospital, he agreed and promised that he would bring a pass for him when he came back to see the boys.

The sergeant turned to the old lady who lived in the castle. "I think we need to close off the entrance to the tunnels. I presume you own the land where the bathing pool is situated. May we have your permission in the interest of public safety to do that?" he asked.

"Certainly, and as soon as possible," she replied, then with a twinkle in her eye she continued, "Mind you, it has all been very exciting!"

"I shall send officers tomorrow to cordon and then seal off both entrances. It will have to be done very quickly, because once the press hear of the prisoner being found there we will have hundreds of people trying to explore a pirate's hide out!"

Once all this was settled, the boys said their 'goodbyes' and 'thank yous' and clambered into Bill's car to go home.

"What am I to do with you boys!" he said. "You are always getting into scrapes! You seem to attract trouble! Thank goodness neither of you were hurt and that you also were able to save that poor man's life. I don't know why he was in prison, but I felt very sorry for him."

Both mothers were so thankful to see their sons safe and well! The whole adventure had to be told once again before the day was over. Finally, when Theo climbed the hundred stairs to his turret bedroom and was ready for bed, he just thanked God for keeping them all safe and helping him not to panic or be afraid. He thought to himself, "I will never forget that verse from Psalm 56, verse 3. 'When I am afraid I will trust in you.' I think it should be my motto for life!"

In the next village, Tyler fell asleep quietly singing 'The Song' to himself.

Chapter Eleven

The half term week was going so quickly! On Wednesday morning the policeman arrived to hear Theo's story. He had already been to see Tyler and heard all about his time in the cavern with the prisoner, and now he needed to record all the details of Theo's escape to find help. It took quite a long time for him to write it all down.

"I seem to remember you boys had an adventure once before, getting shut in a van while thieves were stealing a tractor from Castle View Farm!" the sergeant remarked. "Now, should I put you down as lads who find trouble or lads who are a great help to the police?" he said laughingly. "You had your pictures in the paper then, and I had better warn you that you might make it onto the local news this time, since you saved a man's life and found an escaped prisoner too!"

The policeman turned to Theo's mother: "You may well get the local media asking for interviews. You have every right to refuse them if you feel they will be intrusive in your family's life. Young Theo and Tyler will be local heroes for a while."

"How about the prisoner?" asked Theo, "Is he alright? What will happen to him?"

"He has a very nasty fracture of his leg and was operated on last night. It will take quite a long time to heal. Then he will go back to the Verne prison and will lose some of his remission time for good behaviour. Between you and me, he is not a bad man, just a very sad one who has made some wrong decisions in his life. He hoped to escape and return home to Bulgaria. His knowledge of English is not good, and he is very lonely and isolated in the prison. Your friend's father promises to visit him in hospital, and maybe that will help him. They seem to understand each other's gyspy language a bit, so that will help."

"Good," answered Theo, "We felt sorry for him too. Let's hope he gets better soon."

Later in the day, the media did phone the parents of the two 'T's', asking if they could interview them. Theo's mum talked to Tyler's parents, and they decided that the boys could be interviewed together as long as they were present. That afternoon a very pleasant lady from the Dorset Echo arrived and listened to the boys' story. She took lots of photos and said they would be on the front page of the paper the following day. No sooner had she gone than a film crew arrived from the local TV station. Seb and Flick as well as the two 'T's' were fascinated as the crew set up all their gear. They wanted to know the whole story all over again, but by this time the boys were getting bored with retelling it and just wanted to go off and do something else! The lights were hot, and they felt quite uncomfortable at being portrayed as 'heroes'. "We didn't go out looking for the escaped prisoner," explained Tyler. "We just happened to find our way into the tunnel, and there he was! We only got help just as anyone would have done." Even so, the TV crew seemed to want to make a drama out of it. It was not every day that an escaped prisoner was found at death's door and rescued by two school boys! They filmed for about an hour, and Theo and Tyler were very glad when they went away! They hoped that people would not make too much fuss when they went back to school!

Tyler was much more concerned by some other inhabitants of the cavern which he had discovered when he was left alone with the prisoner. In all the excitement of being rescued, he had forgotten to mention them. Now, having thought more of what the police sergeant had said about sealing off the exit to the cavern, he was becoming worried.

When his eyes had adjusted to the dimness of the cavern, he had become aware that there was a colony of bats on the roof. He had always loved wildlife and was very excited about them and not a bit scared even when they flew around. He didn't know much about bats but was used to observing animals carefully, so he tried to make mental notes in order to identify them. They had pretty long ears (or so he thought, not having seen many bats) and pointed noses. Their faces seemed to be paler in colour, and also the fur on the belly looked white. In the dark it was hard to be sure of their real colour.

After the film crew had gone, he told Theo about the bats, and they decided to look on the internet to see if they were able to identify them. The results were puzzling. Many long words were used and terms they did not understand. The only bat that seemed to answer Tyler's description was the Bechstein's bat, but as it was described as being 'rare', he thought maybe he had got it wrong. He had no idea there were so many species of bats in Britain! The boys decided that they needed to tell someone about the bats. What if they needed to fly out to get their food and now were sealed inside the cavern? Tyler thought his dad would be the first person they should tell.

Tyler's parents were still at the castle, chatting with Theo's mum after all the excitement of the day.

Bill was very interested when Tyler told him about the bats. He thought that the colony may well have been long-eared bats, which were much more common, but they roosted more commonly in trees and buildings. His suggestion was that they contact the Dorset Wildlife Trust, who he was sure would be glad to help. He promised to do that the following day. Since it was almost time for the early evening news broadcast, they all went into the lounge to watch it. After all the time the crew had taken to set up and film the boys, they were a bit disappointed to find the actual time on the TV was only a few minutes. However, they were glad that the story was told accurately, and somehow they both hoped that it would be the end of all the fuss. It had been an amazing adventure, but finding the pirate's pistol and then the pirate's tunnel had been so exciting that they were not sure they wanted to share it with the entire world! However, the filming did show some lovely shots of the Little Syding Castle, and Theo thought that maybe it would help his mum to get more bed and breakfast guests, which would be very good!

After the broadcast, the phone rang. It was the boys' friend Paul, from Castle View farm!

He was very envious of their adventure. Tyler told him about the bats, and Paul said they had some long-eared bats living in one of their barns and invited the boys to go over the next day to see them. That seemed a good idea. Tyler could compare them with the ones he saw in the cavern.

Bill was as good as his word and contacted the Wildlife Trust the following morning. The man he spoke with was very interested. He had heard the news story on the TV the previous evening and wasn't surprised to learn that Tyler had seen bats there. He said that as bats were a protected species he must investigate and so would contact the police that day. Meanwhile, Tyler and Theo cycled over to Paul's home, and he showed them the colony of long-eared bats which lived in their barn. They were so interesting to see.

Tyler could not be really sure if they were the same as he had seen in the cavern. They had long ears and were white underneath, but somehow their faces didn't seem quite the same. Their colour seemed different, but it had been so dark in the cavern.

Paul wanted to hear about the adventure, and they didn't mind telling it again to their friend or to Tim and Tessa, his brother and sister. They knew they wouldn't laugh but would understand that they had prayed when they were scared and that God had been with them and helped them.

It was a long time since they had had a day at the farm, and the boys loved helping with the animals. Even though it was October, there was still plenty to see. Mr Jenkins showed them a few autumn lambs which had been born that week. They were so sweet, skipping around their mothers in the paddock. Mrs Jenkins was about the best cook in the neighbourhood and made a fantastic high tea for them all! The farmhouse kitchen was huge, and she liked nothing better than to have a houseful of young people to feed!

"Are you going to Guy's baptism on Sunday?" Paul asked the two 'T's'.

"Yes, we both have permission to go. We don't know much about it but want to be there to encourage Guy and also learn what it means," said Tyler.

"Dad has promised to take me," said Paul, "I'm sure he'll give both of you a lift too." He looked at his mother. "Can

Theo and Tyler come to tea on Sunday and come with us to the baptism?" he asked.

"That would be lovely! You had better ask your folks and let me know. Come about 4.00 pm, and we'll take you home afterwards. Tim and Tess want to come too, so we'll have to get there early to get a seat!"

The boys cycled home and managed to get in before it was really dark. Soon the clocks would go back, and then the afternoons would be really short! Tyler found his dad had just come home from work.

"I contacted the Wildlife people as I promised, and they went to Portland today. They were allowed to investigate the cavern, and you were right, they are a rare species— Bechstien's bats. They are very excited as they think it is the only known colony in Dorset! Arrangements have to be made so that people cannot enter the passage to the cavern but the bats can still fly out. It seems that won't be too difficult to organise. They will take some photos and later on will invite you and Theo to see them. Seems you will be famous for discovering them as well as saving the prisoner's life! By the way, I have been given permission to visit him too and hope to go on Saturday afternoon. His name is Jakob," Bill added.

"Can I visit him too?" asked Tyler.

"I'm afraid not," replied his dad, "He is still a prisoner, and his room is guarded by a policeman. I have a special pass from the police to visit him. You could write him a letter or a card though. I am sure I could take that to him."

"Ok," said Tyler, trying not to sound too disappointed. "I'll get Theo to write something too."

Chapter Twelve

Sunday arrived, and it was the final day of the half term. The two 'T's' were looking forward to it very much. Both Tyler's and Theo's families now went regularly to church, and the young people all enjoyed being in the 'Live Wires' youth group. Seb and Flick were very enthusiastic about the activities but had not yet decided whether they wanted to give their lives to Jesus and become Christians. When Penny was at home she usually came along, and her musical talents were greatly appreciated helping the worship band. She too had been home for that half term week, but Theo had not spent as much time with her as he really would have liked, partly because of the adventure and partly because Penny spent most of her time practising. She was to play a piano solo at a London concert at Christmas. It was a great honour for her, and she wanted to do it perfectly. After church that day, she was walking home and talking with Theo.

"I really love it at my new school," she was telling him. "I have made some good friends, and we have lots of fun as well as all the focus on music. On Sundays I sing in the Cathedral because I've joined the choir. It's very different from our village church, but I find it awe inspiring. I wish I could believe in God the way you do, but I have many doubts. At school, no one believes the Bible is really true, just a book of myths and morals. How can you believe in Adam and Eve and things like that?" she asked her young brother.

"I'm not very good at answering questions like that," said Theo shyly, "but all I can say is, every time I have sincerely talked to God he has answered me in one way or another. For instance, after I asked him to forgive me for all the hate and anger I felt at Dad leaving us, I felt quite different. I have peace and contentment, and although I still miss Dad, I have forgiven him. Then, another instance is when we were in the cavern this week, a verse we had learnt came to me: 'When I am afraid I will trust in you.' I kept saying it out loud and my terror disappeared, and I was able to think what we should do and then find my way out of the cavern to get help. Every time I have believed what is written in the Bible, I have found it to be true. It seems to me that if some of the Bible is true, then all of it must be. We can't just believe the bits we think are ok, that doesn't make sense. I don't understand much of it, but I am learning more at 'Live Wires' and our 'Faith is Fun' group at school.

"Why don't you come to Guy's baptism tonight, because he is your age and he believes the Bible, even in Adam and Eve, and he's really cool!"

"I'm not sure," replied Penny. "I have to get the early train tomorrow back to Manchester. We were lucky to have an extra day off because the teachers have a training day. If I can get packed in time perhaps I will. Anyway, aren't you going to tea at the Jenkins'? There won't be room for me in their Land Rover."

"Perhaps mum would take you," suggested Theo, "but the twins would have to come too."

Theo really wanted his sister to come to the baptism, so he silently asked the Lord to make a way even though it seemed a bit impossible.

After lunch Tyler walked over to meet Theo so they could continue on walking up to the farm. Theo told him about Penny and how he had prayed that God would make a way for her to come to the baptism.

There was a wonderful smell of baking when they reached the farmhouse! Paul was waiting for them, and the three boys went off to play a computer game together. They had such a good time that they almost didn't hear Mrs Jenkins calling them for tea. The table was loaded with wonderful scones and cakes and home-made bread! There was butter which Tess had churned that day and home-cured ham. It was all delicious! Mr Jenkins came in after finishing the afternoon milking. "I'm running a bit late," he said to his wife. "I wonder if you would drive the children in the Land Rover and I will come as soon as I can in the small car?"

"No problem!" said Mrs Jenkins, smiling. "Shame, we'll have an empty seat now!"

Immediately Theo thought of Penny. "I wonder, Mrs Jenkins, if I could ask Penny if she would like to come. We were talking about it this morning and she was interested but didn't think mum could take her."

"Of course, Theo," replied the farmer's wife. "Why don't you phone and see. We can pick her up on the way."

So it happened that Penny did get to the baptism. They all arrived early at the church and were able to sit near the front. The church was quite different to the village church and had an upstairs balcony. In the front there was a platform, the middle of which had been opened up to make a baptismal pool. The church very quickly filled, and there was a great buzz of excitement. A band were playing and singing songs, some of which the two 'T's' recognised, but others were new to them.

The service began, and the minister explained the meaning of believer's baptism. There were three people being baptised that evening: Guy, a middle aged man and a lady who was quite elderly.

The elderly lady was the first to be baptised. She came forward to the microphone and told everyone that she had always thought she was a Christian simply because she lived in England, which was called a Christian country. She thought that as long as she didn't harm anyone then she stood a good chance of going to heaven. It wasn't until a new neighbour moved into the house next to hers that she learnt that being a Christian meant trusting in Jesus as your Saviour. Her neighbour always helped people in quiet ways and was full of joy, which spilled over to others even though she had experienced many difficulties in her life. When the old lady had asked her how she coped, she learnt about Jesus being alive and real, and after lots of chats she started to come to church. One Sunday she felt the Lord was speaking into her heart, and she gave her life to Jesus. "Not much left of it!" she told everyone with a grin. "I wish I had known Jesus years ago! I might have a job getting in and out of that pool, but my neighbour is going to help me!" Very carefully, her young neighbour helped her into the pool, and the minister and an elder baptised her. Everyone sat in silence as she came out of the water—then they sang a hymn which she had chosen for this special occasion. It was 'Amazing Grace', her favourite. It was very moving, and several people had to wipe away tears!

Next it was the man's turn. His story was quite different. He had been successful in business and climbed to 'the top of the ladder', making lots of money. He had a beautiful home, a wife and two lovely children, but he knew something was missing in his life. He began to drink more than was good for him as well as look in all the wrong places for fulfilment and happiness. Things went wrong in his marriage, and he left his wife. At work he couldn't concentrate and was finally dismissed. His whole successful

life was in tatters. It was then that he found a Bible in a
hotel room and began to read it. It was the beginning of
his search for God. He began to attend church and slowly,
slowly, had come to understand the gospel message of
forgiveness and salvation through Jesus. He had gone back to
his wife and asked forgiveness, and they had been reunited.
Now she too was learning to love Jesus. The church friends
had prayed with him, and he had found another job in a
shop and was so grateful for it. "I had to lose everything
before I thought about God. Now he has changed my life,
and I want to show everyone I am a changed man by being
baptised," he said.

Once again, when he came out of the water, the church
was filled with singing.

Then it was Guy's turn. He was very nervous as he came
to the microphone to tell his story, but once he had begun
his voice became steadier and everyone could hear him
clearly.

"All I remember of my early childhood is a feeling that
I was in the way. My parents often used to shout and then
hit me. One day they disappeared and never came back.
I was taken into care by social services and later fostered
with various families. After a while I was so naughty that
they couldn't cope with me and sent me back to the home.
I grew up angry with everyone and just wanting to lash out
and hit everything and everybody. I tried to be 'hard', but

deep inside I longed for someone to want me and to hug me. I used to look at other kids out with their parents and wondered why mine hated me so much that they walked out on me. By the time I was eight, I was getting into trouble with the police—shop lifting, petty theft, glue sniffing, generally making myself a nuisance. I mucked around at school and was a pain to my teachers!

"I had just started senior school when the social worker told me that a family wanted to meet me, with a view to fostering me. The social worker looked at me quite severely and told me, 'This may be your last chance, Guy. This family know you have caused lots of trouble and are still willing to give you a chance. Don't muck it up!'

"I remember the first meeting with the parents. Well, all I remember is their smiles! They beamed at me as if I were the best-behaved and nicest boy they had ever set their eyes on, not the scum that I had become! Something in me wanted to respond. I wanted them to like me. I wanted to try to be good! Perhaps there was a chance for me in life!

"It was hard at first. They had two older boys and then a small girl with Down's Syndrome. You can't just change and be good. How they had patience with me I shall never know, but they didn't get angry with me and never pushed me away. Their little girl, Angela, was like an angel. She trailed around after me, and I adored her. No one in all my life had just accepted me and loved me even though I was trouble with a big 'T'. The social worker was amazed that I was happy in that home and that the parents wanted to keep me! After I had been there for several months, they asked me if I would like to be adopted and be their own son, because they loved me so much! I broke down and cried like a baby! I began to ask myself why these people were so different and why love filled their house. I knew they went to church because I had been with them. Up until that time I had thought church was for 'sissies' and was just a lot of rubbish. Imagine people believing the Bible was true, things like Adam and Eve, God making the world, Jesus' mother being a virgin! I couldn't see how any intelligent person could believe those things! Yet my mum and dad, for I had begun to call them that, were intelligent and loving and well, absolutely wonderful! I began to ask them questions, and they always took time to answer them. I realised they loved Jesus very much, and he was real to them. Then I began to realise: Jesus loved me, even though I had messed up my life big time. One day it hit me so much, and I realised that Jesus was really the Son of God and had died to take my punishment for all the wrong things I had done. I was in my bedroom and cried and cried and then asked Jesus to forgive me and come into my life. I heard a knock at my bedroom door, and little Angela was there, upset because she had heard me crying. She came in and put her arms around me, and I tried to tell her that everything was fantastic and I loved Jesus, and her face broke into a huge smile!

"Not long after that I was adopted! I now belong to a wonderful family who love me and whom I love. I have also been adopted into God's family, and all my spiritual relations here love and accept me."

Guy looked around at the congregation and beamed at them. "I want to show you all that Jesus has changed me by being baptised. I have chosen as my song Angela's and my favourite, 'I'm special because God has loved me.'"

As he finished, his sister Angela ran out from her seat and gave him a big hug! Then Guy was baptised, and everyone sang his choice of song.

It was such a wonderful service, and the two 'T's' were so glad they had been able to attend.

They had no idea of all the difficulties which Guy had faced in his earlier years. They just looked up to him as the leader of the 'Fif' group.

Theo thought how strange it was that Guy had even talked about the same things as Penny had questioned earlier in the day. He wondered what she had thought of it all. She was very quiet as they left the church.

Chapter Thirteen

The next day Penny left early to return to Manchester. She gave Theo a big hug and whispered to him, "I'm going to really think about becoming a Christian. I've decided to pray that Dad will get in touch with us this Christmas. I know you miss him dreadfully."

Theo and Tyler found they were celebrities when they got back to their year group at school! Almost everybody had seen the TV news where they had been featured. Both boys were a bit embarrassed at all the fuss. The year group tutor asked them a few questions in front of the class, and at least that saved having to repeat the story over and over!

Theo wanted to make sure he had some time in the lunch break to go to the prayer space. He had decided to put Penny's prayer request up on the board so that others would also pray. Guy was coming out of the room, and Theo was glad to tell him how impressed they had been by the service. "Thank you," said Guy quietly. "Please keep on praying for me. The pastor and my parents have warned me that after being baptised it can be a time when you are tested, like Jesus was in the wilderness. Pray I won't let Jesus down."

"I will," answered Theo, "and so will Tyler and Paul when I tell them."

Life soon settled down again, and the boys' lives fell into a routine of school, homework and sport.

There were very few guests coming to visit the castle. Winter was not the time when many people wanted to visit the country, so Theo and the twins didn't need to help much. The chickens and ducks still needed Theo to look after them, and Flick took care of the pony. The swimming pool was drained and cleaned. It was too expensive to heat through the winter, but Theo missed it very much. It was even rather cold in the outhouses, so they didn't bother with snooker or table tennis, except when the youth group came round.

One day Theo came home from school to find his mother was very excited. He wondered what had happened because so often she looked tired and worried.

"I have some interesting news," she said. "I've had a phone call from someone in the department of the environment. You remember seeing the helicopter overhead and we wondered what it was doing? Apparently they were doing surveys of the river. They want to change its course so that it will not cause so much flooding when we get heavy rains. Anyway, a whole group of their officers and engineers want to come and stay here for a couple of weeks while they have discussions and investigations. The part they would like to change runs through our land, so they asked if I would be willing for that to happen. It would be at no cost to us.

When they come they will discuss all that. It's fantastic news for us, because it means we will have enough income to pay the winter bills!"

"That's marvellous, Mum!" said Theo, really pleased for his mother. "Will Tyler's mum be able to help you?"

"Yes, I've already asked her, and she is glad of the work. Even Mrs Jenkins is going to help with some of the baking, because every room will be taken and they may stay quite a while! It will mean you, Seb and Felicity helping a bit with the breakfasts, though."

"Of course we will! It sounds quite exciting. I hope they let us watch what's going on!"

When the 'men from the ministry' (as the two 'T's' dubbed them) arrived, life became full of fun. They were mostly quite young, and Theo's mum decided to open up the games room and fill the swimming pool again, so after they had finished work they were able to enjoy a swim or a game with Theo, the twins and any of their friends who were around. They allowed them all to see what was happening, so long as everyone kept to the rules about keeping their distance from the heavy machinery. The men showed the family the aerial photographs of the river and explained how changing the course would stop it flooding near people's homes. It was a huge undertaking to dig out a new river bed, make high banks and then dam the existing river and divert its course! Many surveys had to be done before the work could begin.

Tyler was very concerned about the otters. No one knew exactly where their setts were. The 'men from the ministry' were very interested in all the wildlife around the river and promised to protect it. The men explained that water voles, otters and toads would all have to be caught and then relocated in the new river. They promised the children that they could help when the time came.

Before the work began, maps were made to show exactly where the river would flow. A large lake would also be formed, from which excess water could be drained when the rainfall was exceptionally heavy.

The thought of a lake in the grounds was exciting! Seb wondered if they could have a rowing boat on it, and Flick suggested that it should be stocked with fish so that it would make the castle an attractive place for anglers to come and stay. Suddenly they were all full of ideas of what could be done to attract more visitors!

It was Tyler who came up with the most brilliant suggestion.

"Why don't you turn the grounds into a sort of small wetlands and wildlife haven? You already have otters, there are lots of fish and crayfish and it would easy to attract water fowl and other birds because we are not far from the sea. You could plant wild flower meadows and then butterflies will come. There will be dragonflies and damselflies! It would be wonderful!"

Everyone could see the potential! What with the ministry paying for all the work and making the lake, with 'nature' taking over, a wildlife centre could be formed in due time.

"We could use one of the barns for a little cafe," suggested Mrs Jenkins, "I could bake for you and even make jams and pickles to sell!"

"I would love to come and help serve teas and coffees!" said Betty, Tyler's mum. "It could be an end to all your worries! You already have good toilet facilities in the swimming pool area, and Bill is very keen on making environmentally friendly toilets which use sawdust or some such thing. He was reading all about them the other day. He learns so much now that he can read!"

There were so many ideas that Theo's mother realised all this was a real possibility. However, she wanted to be sure that it was the right thing to do, so she suggested to her friends that they meet together the following Sunday, when the 'men from the ministry' had gone home for the weekend, to pray together before making any decision. She knew that even if they did decide to go ahead with the idea, it would mean an outlay of cost and also maybe quite a long time before the haven was established. In spite of the possible difficulties, deep in her heart she was very excited about it all!

Chapter Fourteen

Just as he had promised, Tyler's father went to visit Jakob in the hospital. He had to show his police pass each time. Jakob was in a single room, with a prison warden posted outside. At first poor Jakob was very sick and in a lot of pain from his leg as he'd had an operation on it. The five days in the cavern had taken their toll. Each time Bill went to visit him, Jakob's face would light up and he would begin to chatter in his Romany dialect. Bill couldn't understand it all but certainly was able to talk to him a bit. In the course of a few days, they became good friends.

"Thank you for coming. I am so alone here," said Jakob one day. "The nurses just do what they need to do, but they do not speak to me much. I think they all believe I am a dangerous criminal and so keep their distance. Of course, I am a bad man. Otherwise I would not be in prison," he added.

Bill smiled at him. "Why don't you tell me all about it," he said. "If you tell me your story then maybe I will understand why you escaped."

"If I tell you, then you too may not want to visit me again, and I will have nobody," Jakob answered.

"I promise that I will still come and see you and be your friend," answered Bill.

"I am of the Roma people," Jakob began. "Being a Roma yourself, you will also know that many people hate us and think we are bad. In my country, Roma do not get jobs given to them. The children do not go to school. Most of us cannot read or write, and we have few rights as citizens. It makes many of us become bad and have to steal in order to feed our families. It makes us hate the other Bulgarians because we are so marginalised."

Bill nodded. He understood exactly because to some extent the same was true in Britain, and because of this some Romanies had taken to crime.

"I have a wife named Vera and we have seven children— five boys and two girls. I could not feed them. I have no education and no job. I used to sharpen sickles and knives, but people chased us from the door when we tried to ask for work. One day a relative told me he was coming to England because there was work here. I agreed to accompany him. We walked for miles. Sometimes we were able to get lifts in lorries by hiding in them or even under them. Eventually we made our way to France and down to the coast. There a man took all our money and secured us a passage to England, hidden in boxes in a lorry. It was frightening. We could hardly breathe, and we were afraid of being found by immigration officials and sent back home. We were lucky though and were smuggled through the port of Dover. When we reached a service station, we were able to climb out of the lorry. We had no idea where we were. Of course, we now had no money, no passports or documents. The first night we slept under a hedge in a field, and then we began to walk to London.

"We were stupid. We believed that the streets of London were paved with gold! We were sure that if we could just reach that city, somehow everything would be alright. Of course it wasn't! We ended up having to beg for food, or steal it. I stole a blanket one day from a market stall. It was easy to take it without being noticed. I regretted what I had done and felt sad about it all day, yet was so glad to have it that night to keep me warm as I slept under a railway arch. Gradually, I became very good at stealing, and I lost my feelings of being sad about doing such things. Indeed, I became proud of myself that I was so good at it! Then I began to steal so I could sell the stolen goods to make some money.

"One day I was caught! I was brought to the court and found to be an illegal immigrant as well as a thief. Things were very bad for me. They did find someone who spoke Bulgarian to represent me, but I knew he despised me as a Roma and did not care what happened to me. I was sentenced to two years in prison and then to be sent back to my home in disgrace. In that prison I saw myself for the bad man I had become! I had slipped down the slope of stealing so easily! I had even become proud of what I was doing. I was ashamed. What would my poor Vera and my dear children think of me!

"In the prison it all started again! I was ridiculed for being a Roma. I had problems because I could not read or write. I longed for my family. I felt I had to escape and somehow go home and ask for their forgiveness. I needed to know if my Vera would take me back! So I planned for weeks how I could escape. I was used to hiding under lorries and made a plan to hide under the one which came to pick up the furniture we made in the workroom. I did manage to get through the gates, but then the lorry stopped just outside the prison while the driver went for a meal. I guessed that if I stayed in hiding under the lorry, the prison guards would notice I was missing and find me before we moved on, so I ran away. I did not know where I was, except that I was on Portland. I soon found it was a small place, so I looked for a cave by the sea. As I was looking for a place to hide, I found the ruined church and sat down for a rest on a gravestone. To my astonishment, it opened up, and I could see a tunnel! It seemed too good to be true! Then, as I was scrambling down, I fell and broke my leg. The pain was terrible! I was very frightened, especially when I heard the stone move back and I knew I was trapped. Very slowly I made my way crawling along the passage, dragging my broken leg behind me. I do not know how many hours it took me.

"I thought I was going to die. As the days went by I grew weaker. I had nothing with me to eat or drink. I thought not only would I die, but nobody would ever know what happened to me. I had given up hope when the boys arrived. Your son sang to me; it was like an angel visiting me. I knew then that I would live."

Exhausted after telling his story, Jakob turned his face into the pillow and cried silently. Bill was really sad as he listened to the story. He knew how often his own Romany relatives had turned to crime because they were unable to get jobs and felt a despised people. He knew what it was like not to be able to read or write and to feel very powerless. He squeezed his friend's hand and thanked him for sharing his story. Then he began to tell him about 'The Song' and how meeting Jesus had changed their lives. He even told him of the miracle of being given the ability to be able to read.

"Do you think your Jesus would forgive and help me?" asked Jakob.

"I know he will," responded Bill. "I will leave you now to sleep. Think about these things and talk to Jesus about them. He loves you and will answer your prayers."

When Bill arrived home, he shared Jakob's story with Betty and Tyler. Tyler wondered how he could help him, and Bill came up with a good idea.

"He feels the whole world is against him. You know what it was like when you were bullied at the village school because you are a Romany gypsy. Why don't you write him a card and maybe get Theo and Paul to do so too? His room is very bare at the hospital. I am sure cards would cheer him up."

"Thanks, Dad," answered Tyler, "That is a great idea! I'll do one tonight, and I know the others will do some. Maybe the whole 'Fif' group at school would also like to make some, then his room would be very bright! Is it Ok if I share his story so that we can pray for him?"

"I am sure it will be, but I will ask him tomorrow. Don't tell anyone until I have asked him."

Jakob had no objection to the boys hearing his story. "Maybe it will help them to know that stealing is a slippery slope—indeed, all evil is like that. Maybe they will make good choices and not be as stupid as I was! I hope that if I ever see my children again I will be able to teach them not to make bad choices in life. I want to teach them about Jesus now too!" he added, smiling at Bill.

When Tyler told the members of the 'Faith is Fun' group about the prisoner whom they had found, they were very enthusiastic about the idea to send him cards. Bill ended up with a whole bundle, and the hospital room looked so much more cheerful! Jakob was overcome by such kindness. The young people also decided to get him some soap, a facecloth, a toothbrush and toothpaste. They made quite a parcel for him! It all had to be inspected by the prison warden before he was allowed to have it, but it was such a thoughtful gift! They also began to pray for him and for his family. Eventually Jakob was well enough to return to the prison, but Bill continued to visit him each week. Jakob began to attend the prison chapel services and also a Christianity Explored course which was held there. Gradually he began to understand how much Jesus loved him and that his past could be forgiven and he could start a new life. The boys went on sending him cards to cheer him up, and the whole group began to collect things for a Christmas parcel.

Jakob had been rescued and healed in more than one way!

Chapter Fifteen

*A*t the beginning of November, the earth movers and diggers arrived. Now only one 'man from the ministry' remained at the castle to supervise the work, but the house still remained full of guests because the workmen moved in. It was amazing how quickly the work advanced! After school each day, the two 'T's' ran through the meadow to see the progress. The channel for the river was very deep, and at first all went well, until the workmen had a surprise because they found a skeleton! All the work had to stop while investigations were made. At first it involved the police, but they quickly realised this was an ancient skeleton, and so the archaeologists were called in. Gradually a whole lot of Roman remains were discovered. A large tent was erected over the site while there were consultations about what should be done next. Many people gathered to inspect the site, and thermal images were taken from the skies which were able to reveal just how big the area was that needed investigating. The boys found it fascinating. The work on the new river bed stopped for a couple of weeks. Its course had to be changed slightly in order to leave the archaeological site intact.

It was decided that the archaeologists would begin work in the new year, as long as it didn't freeze or snow too much. A team would be sent from Oxford University to work on the site, and they promised that the boys and Flick could help if they wished. Theo was very excited about this.

Tyler was more interested in the development of the conservation and wildlife area. As soon as the new river bed was prepared, some of the existing wildlife was captured, weighed and inspected for good health. Once the river was dammed and allowed to flow into the new channel, the animals were returned, and it was hoped they would make new homes. A very large lake had been dug out, which was for collecting any excess water in times of flooding. It also had a sluice gate which, when required, could be used to safely release excess water. In the centre of the lake, an area had been preserved where a couple of old willow trees stood. This was to be a small island. The banks of the river had been carefully graded, and the boys helped plant new wetland plants to stop erosion. Whenever they had any free time, they were out in their wellies having a marvellous time in the mud! Paul and his brother Tim often came down from Castle View farm to help. Their father brought his plough and dug up a whole field. Wild flower meadow seeds were planted. They hoped it was not too late in the year but decided it was worth trying. The beginnings of the wildlife park had started! It would take a long time to become established, but it was great to see it all taking shape. The twins, the two 'T's' and the three children from Castle View farm decided to form their own WildLife Society. Tyler was to be the president because he was the most knowledgeable. They agreed to meet on Saturday afternoons whenever possible, and each of them would keep wildlife diaries of all the birds, animals and wild flowers they saw. They shared the books they already had about British wildlife and also borrowed some from the library. They were very surprised at how many species they could find, even in wintertime. The 'man from the ministry' encouraged them and recorded anything he saw as well. Their observations would be valuable information as the wetlands area developed. They all enjoyed having something interesting to do through the winter months, even when the weather was bad.

Once December had arrived, everyone began to plan for Christmas. The 'Wildlife Society' decided they would put on a sort of 'Wind in the Willows' pantomime for their families. It was just a fun thing. Seb wrote the script, and they made paper animal masks to wear. The practices were usually held in the barn at Castle View farm and often ended up with 'hay fights' and much laughter!

At school the members of the 'Fif' group all wrote Christmas cards for Jakob and saved up to buy him small gifts. They were really pleased to hear that he was learning about Christianity through the Christianity Explored course and prayed that he would understand all he was taught and come to love Jesus as his Saviour. Bill had become his friend, and Jakob looked forward to his weekly visits. Bill wondered if he might become an authorised 'Prison Visitor', as that way he could meet other prisoners and maybe help them too. Meeting Jakob had shown him that prisoners were people with needs. Many of them had made wrong choices and got their lives into a mess but were now lonely and isolated. Tyler's family also began to write to Jakob's family in Bulgaria, using their Romany language. They hoped that they could find somebody who could read and understand it. They made up a Christmas parcel with sweets and small gifts for his wife and seven children. It was good to be able to help the family he loved so much.

Chapter Sixteen

Theo was sitting one day in the 'prayer space' at school and asking God to do a miracle for him. He was praying that his father would come home and hear Penny give her concert in Wigmore Hall in London. It was going to be the most important day of her life, and Theo knew how much she wanted her dad to be there. Of course, it seemed impossible! He was thousands of miles away in Australia, and now he had a new family. He wondered what his little half sister was like. Perhaps she was like Tyler's baby sister Sunshine, who made them all laugh when she toddled around. Sunshine loved to wear hats! Now it was winter she grabbed the two 'T's' hats and tried to wear them, but as they were too big her eyes were covered and she would end up falling over and making everyone laugh! She was such fun!

As he was sitting and thinking he realised that as well as praying there was something else he could do! Why hadn't he thought of it before? His mother had Dad's address because very occasionally he sent her a little support money. He could write to his father! He would at least tell him about the concert, send him a Christmas card and even tell him the news about the river and archaeological dig.

Somehow, as these ideas came to him in the 'prayer space', he felt sure that it was God who had put them into his mind. When he was on the school bus going home, he mentioned it to Tyler. He shared everything with his best mate. Tyler thought it was a brilliant idea. Once they were home, Theo asked his mum for his father's address. She looked at him searchingly, not wanting her son to be hurt if he didn't get a reply. She knew how very much her children had already been hurt by their father's rejection.

"I want to send him a Christmas card," Theo told his mum. He decided not to tell her about the concert because it was like a prayer secret between him and Penny.

"Alright then. Be careful though, don't get upset if doesn't reply," said his mother as she went to her cupboard and wrote out the address. Theo tucked it into his pocket.

"Thank you, Mum," he answered. "Don't worry, I know he probably won't reply, but I would like him to get a card anyway."

The boys went upstairs to do their homework. They had made a rule to always do this first before any other activity. They helped each other, or to be more accurate, Theo helped Tyler, who was still trying to catch up on the years he had lost when they were travellers and he didn't go to school. At 'prep' school, Theo had learnt French. This meant he was top of the first division and able to help Tyler who struggled with English, let alone French! However, Tyler was intelligent and learnt quickly. Theo was sure he would soon catch up.

After homework Tyler's father stopped by on his way home from work to pick him up. Now that it was dark so early in the evenings, he was glad of the lift. Once he had gone, Theo began to write to his dad.

"Dear Dad," he began. "I hope you and your wife and baby Lucy Jane are well." Then he sucked the top of his pen for ages, not quite knowing how to write all that he wanted to say. "I like my senior school. We are learning lots of new things, and I have joined several clubs. My best friend is Tyler, who lives in a cottage in the woods at Much Syding. We had a big adventure together at half term when we visited a cove at Portland. Lots of things are happening at home too, because the ministry for the environment have changed the course of the river. We now have a lake and an island.

"Seb and Flick are fine. We still like to swim a lot when we can, and all of us are in the school swimming squad. Penny is away at music school, and I miss her lots. We are excited because she has a concert at Wigmore Hall in London on December 16th. We are all going to hear her play.

"Please have a lovely Christmas and don't forget about us. After all, you are our dad, and we love you."

Theo paused after writing this. He hoped it was alright to say that, because it was true.

Then he finished the letter:

"With love, from Theodore."

His dad had always called him by his full name, so he thought he should sign it that way.

He put the letter and card into the envelope and stuck it down. He didn't really want anyone else to read it. He copied the address his mother had given him on to the envelope, then carefully put that piece of paper away. His heart felt heavy. He did miss his dad, and he did love him!

His mum gave him an airmail sticker and promised to post it the next day. It was almost supper time, so Theo helped his mother lay the table and tried to be grateful that he had his mum and his brother and sisters. He thought of Guy, who was not wanted by his natural family at all, and of the awful time when he was in care or in foster homes. He was glad Guy now had an adopted family who loved him.

Within a few days, the weather became really wintry. In the mornings, the frost was thick and there was ice on the new lake. The 'man from the ministry' and all the workmen had now left. When Theo went to feed his chickens and ducks, his wellies scrunched through frosted grass. He always took his notepad and pencil and was amazed at how many interesting birds he saw. A whole flock of redwings invaded the paddock. Theo wasn't sure he had seen any before but learnt they were winter visitors to the area. The weatherman on the radio forecasted a 'white' Christmas. If that happened, the children had all already planned to have fun sledging over the fields. Dorset didn't often get snow, so they would have to make the most of it! Theo was looking forward to the Christmas holidays. The pantomime that the 'Wildlife Society' had written was going to be great fun. The three families planned to be together on Boxing Day for a party at the castle, and they would perform it then. There was a lot to look forward to. First, however, there was the concert in London. Mum had explained to the school that Seb, Flick and Theo would need some time off as they had to travel early in the day in order to be in time for the concert and that they would need to stay overnight because it ended quite late. The children were pleased that they were going to stay with their Auntie Jane, their mother's younger sister. She had a tiny house in the London suburbs, so this meant they would be sleeping on the floor. They didn't mind at all as she made it such fun.

The day of the concert was very cold and frosty. The family decided to catch the early train so that they could see some of the London sights. Even the journey to London was interesting as the train wound its way slowly along the coast to Southampton and then quicker from there to London.

Everywhere looked Christmassy! There were even men selling hot chestnuts on the streets of London! First they visited the docklands, and this was followed by going to the

West End to see the lights in Oxford and Regent Streets.
They found a nice place to eat and even had time for a little
Christmas shopping. Theo was very pleased because he
found a wildlife book for Tyler and a fluffy owl for Sunshine.
He wondered what he could get for Paul, Tim and Tess.
Eventually he decided on a London mug for each of them.
When they had finished shopping, their mother took them
to a restaurant near Wigmore Hall. It was a great treat to
choose something from a menu. Their mum told them they
deserved a treat because they had all helped her so much
with the bed and breakfast business and happily taken on
extra jobs when Penny had left for her new school. After
they had eaten, she sent them all to the restrooms to change
and make themselves as smart as possible before they went
to the concert.

The concert hall was decorated with red poinsettias and
looked very festive. Lots of people were arriving, and there
was a buzz of anticipation. Several of the young people
from the Manchester Music School were performing solos,
and the choir were also singing carols. Theo looked at the
programme and felt very proud to see:

'Beethoven's *Moonlight Sonata*   Miss Penelope Russell'

He wondered if he could ask for another programme. He
wanted to send one to his father but also wanted to keep
his own copy. He was thinking about this when suddenly
there was a hush and the lights were dimmed. The

orchestra began to play the national anthem, and everyone stood up to sing.

The programme began. It was all very interesting, but Theo couldn't wait to see his big sister! She had to wait until almost the very end to perform. That must have been scary for her! Theo found himself quietly asking God to give her courage and help her to remember all the notes. He knew that she worried about getting things wrong and was nervous in front of crowds.

When it was her turn he felt like his chest would burst with pride! She looked beautiful in a long dark blue dress and her long fair hair tied back with a blue bow. Theo could tell she was nervous because her head was a little on one side and she always held it like that when she was tense. Once she began playing, the piano the whole hall was filled with the beautiful music. It almost made Theo cry. He had a big lump in his throat! Penny did so well, and there was a thunderous applause at the end. She got up and took her bow. As she looked up, it was as if she saw something very special, because a wonderful smile spread over her face!

At the end of the concert, when people were beginning to move from their seats, someone ruffled Theo's hair. It sent a shiver down his spine. It wasn't … it couldn't be … but it was!

Chapter Seventeen

"Dad!" exclaimed Theo. "Dad, is it really you?" He looked at his dad, drinking in all the features he loved so well yet had found difficult to recall.

"Yes, son," answered his father softly. "It's really me!" Suddenly he was being hugged by Theo and the twins all at once.

"Steady on! Let me breathe!" he laughed. Theo's mum, Sally, was looking pale and shocked.

"I'm sorry," said Dad. "I shouldn't have sprung this on you without warning, but part of me wanted to surprise you. I had very little notice that I was to come to Europe. I have a meeting in Amsterdam, and when I got young Theo's card telling me about the concert, I thought I must come over. I was so proud to be here and see Penny perform so beautifully and then have the opportunity to see all my children again. There is something I want to say to you all, but I'll wait until Penny joins us. Sally, I'm sorry if I gave you a shock," he said, turning to their mother. "I didn't want to hurt you again."

Soon Penny joined the family. She was beaming from ear to ear. "Dad, I just couldn't believe it when I took my bow and suddenly saw you in the audience! It's fantastic to see you!" And she gave her father a huge hug.

"Let's go somewhere quiet and have a drink," their father suggested. "That is, if you have time."

Their mother nodded. "We can spare about an hour. We are staying the night with Jane. I'll just text her to say we will be a bit later than we thought."

The family left the theatre and found a coffee shop where they could talk. When everyone had ordered their drinks, their father began to speak.

"I have longed so much to see you all and tell you face to face how sorry I am that I have caused you all so much hurt. Your mother and I had not been happy together for quite a long time, and I must tell you that it was my fault, not hers. I can never undo the hurt I have inflicted, and I am terribly sorry for that. The way I handled things was very wrong, and I am ashamed. Even when Linda and I reached Australia and settled there, I should have been a better father and provided for you all. You had been used to a lifestyle that I could no longer afford, but I should have found some way to help you all manage. Instead I was a coward and left you to cope alone. For that I am deeply sorry. I deserted you children and didn't deserve the welcome you gave me. I hope one day you will all be able to forgive me. I now have a better job, and it is my promise that I will help you all as much as possible. I know I have not been a very good dad, so you may find that hard to believe, but I do promise you."

There was a silence, and no one seemed to know quite what to say. They sipped their drinks, trying to take in their father's apology. It was their mother who spoke first.

"You know we have turned the castle into a bed and breakfast business. All of the children work very hard helping me, especially in the summer."

Suddenly everyone was talking. They told their father about the hens and ducks, the church using the premises for social activities, the ministry for the environment and the change of the river's course, the new wildlife park they were hoping to make and the excavations of the Roman remains. It was hard for him to take it all in as everyone was talking at once! Now they were all laughing together. Theo felt his father ruffle his hair again. He looked up. "What about you, young man. What adventures have you been having?"

"You'll be here all night, Dad!" said Seb. "Theo's always having adventures with his friend Tyler!" They laughed again, and then Theo answered his dad.

"Yes, I've had lots of adventures and lots of fun. I think I had better write and tell you all those. Will you write back? And have you got a photo to show us of our little sister, Lucy Jane?"

"I surely have!" answered their father and pulled out his wallet. They all looked at the photo that showed a dear little baby girl in a frilly dress. She had a lovely smile that made her look a bit like Penny. "Here is another one. Her mother,

Linda, is holding her." They saw a slim young woman in jeans and T-shirt with long blonde hair. Theo thought she looked kind, and he was glad of that.

"Now I must go as I have to catch the Eurostar train," said their father. He looked at their mum and asked, "I really would like to keep in touch properly. I know it's a lot to ask after the way I have treated you all, but would you allow me to talk to you on Skype each week? We could arrange a schedule that would suit you."

Their mum nodded. "I think it would be good. The children need to talk to their dad regularly. They have missed you so much."

Just before he left for his train, their father pulled out four envelopes from his pocket.

"These are Christmas cards from 'down under'. Keep them until Christmas day." Then he hugged his children one by one and reassured them of his love. He was wiping away tears as he left the cafe.

"Are you alright, Mum?" Theo asked as they picked up their belongings and headed towards the underground to catch a train to their aunt's home. "I know you said I could write, but I didn't dream that dad would come to the concert. I wouldn't have hurt you for anything!"

"Don't worry, please," replied his mum as she looked at all her children. "I want you to know that although I was very hurt when your dad left home, since I have become a

Christian I have been able to forgive him and also myself for
the mess we made of our marriage. It always takes two to
make or break a marriage. I have been praying that one day
you would all have contact with your father, and now it has
happened. I was shocked to see him but so happy for you
all, especially for Penny, that he could see her do so well! We
were all very proud of you tonight, my dear."

Penny sat next to Theo in the tube train.

"You told him about the concert, didn't you?" she
commented.

"Yes, I did, when I sent him a Christmas card. I promised
to pray and asked God for a miracle for you, that Dad would
be at your concert. I left it in the 'prayer space' at school,
so I guess others would have prayed too. Then I suddenly
realised that I had a part to play too. I asked Mum for Dad's
address and wrote a card, not asking him to come but telling
him all about when and where the concert was."

"This has helped me believe that there really is a God who
loves us and hears our prayers!" she answered. "Thank you,
Theo. You are the best young brother in the world!"

Theo grinned. "And you're the best big sister! I can't wait
to tell Tyler what's happened!"

Coming soon in the Syding Adventures

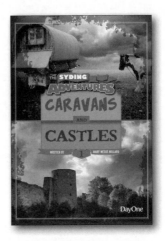

CARAVANS AND CASTLES (1)

Mary Weeks Millard

ISBN 978-1-84625-364-5

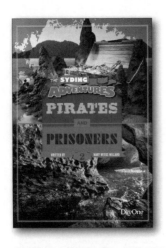

PIRATES AND PRISONERS (2)

Mary Weeks Millard

ISBN 978-1-84625-365-2

SUNSHINE AND SNOWSTORMS (3)

Mary Weeks Millard

ISBN 978-1-84625-366-9

ROMANS AND RANSOMS (4)

Mary Weeks Millard

ISBN 978-1-84625-367-6

LIVE WIRES AND LOBSTER POTS (5)

Mary Weeks Millard

ISBN 978-1-84625-368-3

VIKINGS AND VISITORS (6)

Mary Weeks Millard

ISBN 978-1-84625-369-0

HOLIDAYS AND HIJACKINGS (7)

Mary Weeks Millard

ISBN 978-1-84625-370-6

If you enjoyed these you might like the following books by Mary Weeks Millard

THE SECRET OF THE HIDDEN TUNNEL

Mary Weeks Millard

ISBN 978-1-84625-334-8

NEVER GIVE UP ON YOUR DREAMS

Mary Weeks Millard

ISBN 978-1-84625-271-6

THE MYSTERY OF THE DESERTED HOUSE

Mary Weeks Millard

ISBN 978-1-84625-272-3

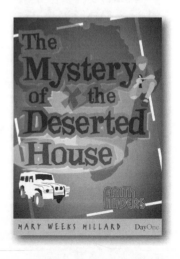